A TRIBE
FOR LEXI

A TRIBE FOR LEXI

C. S. ADLER

Macmillan Publishing Company   New York
Collier Macmillan Canada   Toronto
Maxwell Macmillan International Publishing Group
New York   Oxford   Singapore   Sydney

Macmillan Publishing Company
866 Third Avenue
New York, NY 10022

Collier Macmillan Canada, Inc.
1200 Eglinton Avenue East
Suite 200
Don Mills, Ontario M3C 3N1

First edition
Printed in the United States of America
10   9   8   7   6   5   4   3   2   1

The text of this book is set in 12 point Berkeley O.S.
Book design by Christy Hale

Library of Congress Cataloging-in-Publication Data
Adler, C. S. (Carole S.)
A tribe for Lexi / by C.S. Adler.—1st ed.
p.   cm.
Summary: While spending the summer at her cousin's farm in upper
New York State, twelve-year-old Lexi finds that, of all her cousins,
only withdrawn eleven-year-old Jeb offers her friendship, and Lexi
decides to help him attain his heart's desire.
ISBN 0-02-700361-2
[1. Cousins—Fiction.   2. Interpersonal relations—Fiction.
3. Survival—Fiction.   4. Indians of North America—Fiction.]
I. Title.
PZ7.A26145Tr   1991   [Fic]—dc20
90-6322   CIP   AC

To Arnie, my husband, helpmate, companion, beloved

With thanks to Ceil Mack, storyteller *extraordinaire,*
who generously gave me this one.
With thanks also to Louis Wichinsky who provided details
of the Catskill Mountains flora and fauna.

A TRIBE
FOR LEXI

Lexi hoped to fit right in here in her cousins' house this summer, to feel instantly at home. It wouldn't be like the boarding school Dad had sent her to where they'd labeled her an oddball and ignored her. It wouldn't be like the countries they'd lived in where she had to learn a new language and where people ate and dressed and thought differently from her. Here they were family, her family.

But when she woke up the first morning, it was late and both her girl cousins had left the attic bedroom. Nothing in it looked familiar, not even the star-patterned quilts on their beds. Considering that the quilts were the only beautiful objects in the long, bare attic room, Lexi was puzzled that she didn't remember them. This was the room she'd slept in on that Christmas weekend visit two and a half years ago. Unless the quilts were new. She studied them for clues. They looked like their owners. Janet's was somber with lots of dark blue squares, while Jesse's was dusty pink and flowery looking. Well, Janet was a somber fifteen-year-old, heavyset and older in her ways than her mother. Janet had greeted Lexi formally last night, and her dark, intelligent eyes had reserved judgment. Jesse on the other hand had kissed Lexi and called her cousin.

"It's going to be such fun having another girl around this summer," Jesse had said. "You'll even up our side against the boys." Her plump cheeks dimpled and she had a pink peony look like her quilt. Jesse was thirteen, just a year older than Lexi. Why didn't she like Jesse best, Lexi wondered? Jesse was easy, but she preferred Janet so far. Serious people. She had always liked serious people.

She slipped out of bed and walked barefoot across the smoothly varnished wood floor to the only window. The sunshine filling it overflowed into the room. Outside Lexi could see the barn and the big trees that shaded the road. She had been dreaming of exploring this peaceful Catskill countryside for months now. No gun-toting soldiers would march into this yard. And the ghost of the houseboy they had killed wouldn't haunt her here. She breathed deeply of the fragrant summer air. She had finally landed in a place where she belonged.

Suddenly two of her three boy cousins dashed into the yard. "I'm sorry. I'm sorry," skinny Jeb yelled as he ran from his big, fourteen-year-old brother, Jim. A few feet from the barn, Jim caught up with Jeb and *whack*. Down came what looked like a bicycle inner tube on Jeb's back. Lexi couldn't believe it. Jim was using all his ballplayer's muscular strength in the beating he was giving his younger brother, but Jeb barely grunted as the strap came down again and again.

"Stop that, you stop that," Lexi screamed. She unhooked the screen so that she could lean out to get Jim's attention. Nothing happened. Either her voice hadn't carried or Jim didn't care what she said. His rubber weapon hissed and slapped against the thin back now crouched at his feet. The sound made her cry out even though Jeb was silent.

"Told you not to touch my lucky ball. Told you, didn't I?" *Whack*. Jeb's head jerked.

"You stop that, you big bully," Lexi screamed at Jim.

This time he heard her and looked up at the window. "Shove it," he said. "It's none of your business what I do to my brother."

"He's my cousin, and you better stop or you'll be sorry," she threatened.

Jim grinned at that. She didn't care if he was amused by her threat so long as he stopped. Barefooted, in the knee-length T-shirt she slept in, she raced downstairs and reached the front porch in time to witness the last of the beating.

"Next time you wanna use something of mine, you ask," Jim told Jeb. He smacked the bicycle inner tube against his own hand in one last blast of temper.

She ran to Jeb. "Did he hurt you?"

Jeb rolled up like a snail facing away from her.

She turned on Jim. "What did he do that was so awful?"

"Hey, what's it to you? You're just visiting, remember? You're not part of the family."

"I am too part of this family." She stepped toward him, head cocked and hands set on her narrow hips. She was too angry to consider how ridiculous she must look challenging him until she saw his reaction.

First he looked amazed. Then he laughed and raised his big hands palms out. "Don't hit me," he begged in a fake scared voice, "I surrender." She felt foolish. He was tall and muscular. She was reed thin and small, two years younger than he was.

She pushed her long brown hair back from her narrow face and said with all the dignity she could muster, "I hate brutality." She had seen enough of it in the village near the power plant Dad was helping to build in West Africa. She hadn't seen their houseboy killed, but she had seen a child's body the soldiers had left by the well as a warning.

But Jim didn't know that. He said, "You know what, Cousin? It don't matter one bit to me what you hate." And just to show her, he raised his work boot and kicked Jeb in the back.

She screamed in sympathetic pain as Jim walked away. "Jeb," she said, "don't move. I'll get help."

"No. Leave me be," Jeb muttered. "I don't need help."

"But he hurt you."

"No, he didn't. I lost his baseball, the one Hank Aaron signed."

She squatted beside him considering what to do. "Who's Hank Aaron?" she asked absentmindedly.

Jeb rolled over and looked up at her with surprise. "You don't know?"

He was so cross-eyed that Lexi kept shifting her gaze, uncertain of how to return his look. "No," she said. "In Africa and South America where we've lived, soccer's the big sport."

Jeb considered. Finally he said, "Well, Jim had a right to be mad. That ball meant a lot to him."

"Is that why you didn't cry?"

"No. You can't cry if you're an Indian."

"And you're an Indian?"

"Well, not yet, but I'm practicing." He began easing himself upright.

"You're bleeding," she said, seeing a bloody line on the back of his shirt. "You better show your mother your back."

"Mom's gone to work."

That was news. It helped explain why Lexi had barely recognized her Aunt Jane at the train station last night. "My new hairdo," Aunt Jane had said, but more than her hair had changed. "Where's she working?"

"She got the tax collector job last month while Dad was laid off. Now he's back in the mill, but Mom says she likes her job too much to give it up."

"So who takes care of you and Joe?" Joe was the youngest boy. He was only eleven.

"Jim does, or Janet and Jesse. But I can take care of myself. Mostly Jim takes care of Joe because they both play baseball."

"All the time?"

"Most of the time. Leastways in the summer." He sat up cautiously. "What was it like living in Africa? I've never been farther than town."

What was it like? She thought of the sky so vast it made her feel helpless, and the women swaying patiently along the road to market with their produce in baskets on their heads and their babies slung in cloth to be car-

16

ried, too. Laughter and the dreadful quiet of the sick and dying. "Mostly it was pretty lonely. The last place we lived I even had to do lessons by myself without a regular teacher. I couldn't even leave the compound because of the soldiers." He looked puzzled. "Well, they hadn't been paid so they were dangerous," she explained, and then because he was still listening, she went on.

"We've never lived anywhere where I could wander alone. In Brazil, where Dad was a construction manager before this job, half the wildlife was poisonous. It wasn't even safe to swim in the river." She looked around. The leaves were whispering in the breeze, but everything else was still and soft.

"We've got rattlers," Jeb said. "Well, I've never seen one, but there's supposed to be some left in the mountains."

She smiled. The plump hills he called mountains looked tame as house cats to her. "Your brother Jim's the worst thing you tangle with around here, I bet," she said.

"He's not so bad." Jeb stood up. He was taller than Lexi. Most people were, although she liked to think of herself as tall and always stood very straight. "I'm okay," he said. "Thanks for trying to help me though. You were pretty brave." He nodded at her and walked off toward the house, moving stiffly as if he hurt.

Where had he been in that happy Christmas weekend she'd spent here? She remembered Janet and Jesse help-

17

ing their mother bring in the endless platters of delicious-smelling food, sweet potatoes and candied carrots and corn pudding and beans with almonds and the crisp-skinned turkey. She remembered Jim lifting Joe up to reach an ornament near the top of the ceiling-high tree. And the laughter and teasing. They had all seemed so happy together. After dinner Janet had played the piano for the Christmas carols they sang together. "You sing the high parts with me," Jesse had told Lexi. Then Jim and Joe had taken her out to the barn to show her the owl. They were feeding it until its wing healed. Jeb? Where had Jeb been? Absorbed in the toy train that ran around a cloth mountain and past a miniature town under the tree, that was her only image of him.

Nobody but Jeb was in the kitchen. He stood at the sink, stripped to the waist, washing the blood out of his T-shirt. His rib cage showed through his pale skin. His back was welted, but blood only oozed from one broken line.

"You need some antiseptic on that," she said.

"No, it's okay. Could you maybe wipe off the blood for me?"

She dabbed at his back with wet paper toweling as gently as she could.

"Thanks," Jeb said, when she stopped. He opened the refrigerator and got out a container of milk. "Want some?"

She shook her head. "How come you took his ball?" she asked.

"He told me to bring it home after the game."

"Maybe we can find it. I mean, we could retrace your steps."

"Too late. Someone's got it by now. Anyway, Jim won't be mad at me anymore. He's paid me back."

"You're not mad at him for beating you up like that?"

"Why should I be? . . . Listen," Jeb confided, "I got to tell you, if you want them to like you, you better not bother with me. Nobody bothers with me in this family." He put his wet T-shirt back on and walked out of the house, leaving her alone in it.

She stared after him in wonder. Could Jeb have grown up with brothers and sisters and still be an outsider? She had always envied people with large families. Sure they might complain about one another and squabble, but they belonged to a tribe and that was what she wanted most.

Sorrowfully, she thought of Ezekiel, the gentle, small-boned houseboy who'd been her friend. Once he had caught a lizard for her to keep as a pet, and one misty morning he'd taken her to the lake to see long-legged birds take flight in a thrilling rush of wings. It was after the soldiers killed him that her father had insisted on shipping her off to a school in the States, to Thistlewood Academy. "We want you to be safe," her father had said.

"But you won't be safe. And Mother. You're staying here. Why can't I?"

"I promised to finish this job, Lexi. As for your mother, she says her job is to be with me. *Your* job is to grow up healthy."

He hadn't given her a choice. He had made the arrangements and sent her away.

"What are you crying about?" her roommate had asked her the first night at Thistlewood. "Are you homesick?"

"No," Lexi had told her, "I'm crying for Ezekiel." And she had described how he had been killed. She had explained how his tales about the blind chief of his village, and his mother whose big heart made her everybody's mother, and his little sister with the flirting eyes, had made Lexi care, not just for him, but for his whole village. She had only visited the village once, but the people had welcomed her with a warmth that made her imagine briefly that she could belong with them.

Her own mother wasn't warm. Her own mother hid from Lexi deep inside herself. She behaved as if Lexi were competing with her for her husband's affection. Lexi had confided all that in a torrent of words while the roommate listened, wide-eyed, half of the first night at Thistlewood. But she hadn't explained very well, or else her roommate hadn't understood, because soon Lexi heard whispers about her—that she had loved a servant, an African man, that she'd been sent away to school because she had loved him and he'd been killed.

It hadn't been just the rumors that had made them think she was strange. Her clothes had been wrong, too. Because she was so slight, her mother bought her children's sizes, no designer labels, just plain catalog department-store skirts and pants and tops. Then she was always roaming off in the woods alone and showing up late for class. She knew how to recognize a chickadee's *phoebe* call, but she failed every math quiz no matter how hard she studied. "Weird," they said when she tried out for the boys' soccer team. She was good at soccer. She was good with a ball. But she hadn't been admired for that or for anything else at Thistlewood.

Well, she'd learned her lesson. Here she would find out what Janet and Jesse were like, and that was how she would be. She would watch how they acted and behave as they did. She would join in with the things they liked to do. Coming to Aunt Jane's farm had been Lexi's idea when her father suggested camp for this summer. "They're my cousins," she had said, remembering how they had called her "Cousin Lexi" that long ago Christmas. The words held a promise, and now she was here.

2

Jeb slipped back into the kitchen and got a ruler and a pencil from a drawer. Before he left again, Lexi asked, "Will Janet and Jesse get home soon?"

"They went down to the church. They're always doing something at the church," Jeb said. "Probably they'll be back for lunch."

Alone again, Lexi shivered in the cool of the kitchen and decided she'd get dressed. The only mess she saw anywhere in the attic bedroom was the clothes spilling from her hastily opened suitcase. She repacked it. There didn't seem to be any better place to keep her clothes. There. Now her end of the room looked neat, too.

She checked out the bulletin board between the two maple dressers: birthday cards, notices about choir practice and a church picnic, a picture of a basketball player from a newspaper that turned out to be not a boyfriend, but Jim. There was a photograph of a big, mixed-breed dog labeled "our faithful Wolfie," and a picture of Janet and Jesse arm in arm in shorts and baggy T-shirts. Lexi wondered if it bothered them to be so broad and beefy when their brothers were slim and good-looking. Well, Jim and Joe were good-looking. Jeb wasn't really.

The morning was half over. Lexi sat nibbling on a bran muffin at the long, wooden kitchen table. She didn't know where Jeb was. If Jesse and Janet didn't show up soon, what she would do was explore on her own. She was eager to discover the landscape, to become familiar with the river's whims and the woods' secrets. That kind of reading was even more enjoyable than books to her.

Too bad they didn't still work the farm. She had imagined apple picking and pitching hay into a truck bed. She had imagined reaching under the feathery breast of a clucking hen to retrieve a warm egg. But Aunt Jane had said that not only had they gotten rid of the cow when Uncle Jake went to work at the mill full-time, but also the chickens. No matter. Lexi was game for whatever they still did.

She was cleaning the crumbs off the table when her aunt walked in with Janet and Jesse. "So you woke up,

Alexandra. Have a good sleep?" Aunt Jane asked heartily.

"I don't usually sleep that late. I guess I was tired."

"Well, you had a long trip. I'm sorry we wasn't home to welcome you, but I had to get to work and the girls had a committee meeting. I took the afternoon off, though. The boys treat you right?"

"Uh—yes, okay." It would sound like tattling to blurt out that her only contact with the boys had been while Jim was beating Jeb up.

"I bet Jim took off for the ball field before Lexi got up, Ma," Janet said. "Him and Joe don't miss a minute they can get playing ball in the summer."

"Is that right, Lexi?" Aunt Jane asked. And without waiting for an answer, she asked, "Where's Jeb?"

"I don't know. He was here a little while ago," Lexi said.

"Umm. Probably in the barn. He practically lives in the barn. That boy should have been a cat."

"Or a mouse," Jesse said. She and her mother laughed.

Janet was opening a can of tuna fish. Jesse had put bread and glasses on the counter. "We take care of ourselves for breakfast and lunch mostly," Janet said. "Just grab what we feel like. Want me to make you a tuna fish sandwich?"

"No thank you. I ate a muffin."

"You don't look like you eat much," Aunt Jane said. "This family's all big eaters, but it goes right off the boys and sticks to me and the girls." She laughed. "Last fall we went to Weight Watchers together. Janet and Jesse and me lost a total of fifty pounds."

"Fifty-six, Mama," Janet said.

"Well, we put it back on fast enough. Are you a fussy eater, Alexandra?"

"Oh, no. I eat everything," Lexi hastened to assure her. "Just not a lot of everything."

The tuna fish sandwiches Janet made were as ample as the three people who sat down to eat them. Lexi wondered why the sisters were wearing identical sweatshirts, except that Janet's was blue and Jesse's was pink. Would she be expected to show up in a happy-faced sweatshirt, too? Jesse smiled at Lexi, showing pretty teeth. Janet watched, chewing quietly. Lexi was watching, too, for clues to how to behave so that they would like her. She hoped not eating a lot wouldn't count against her.

"We're going to the mall later. We got to get fabric for a quilt we're making for the church's centennial. Want to come?" Janet asked her.

"Sure," Lexi said gladly. "A quilt? You didn't make the ones on your beds, did you?"

"We sure did. Last winter," Janet said. "Jesse and me like to quilt."

"Can you sew?" Jesse asked.

"Well, not very much. I've never learned. My mother does all kinds of needlework, but she likes to do things

25

alone. She. . ." Lexi couldn't go any farther without accusing her mother of an unwillingness to share her pleasures with her only child, although that happened to be the way it was. She stopped talking.

"You can't sew?" Jesse sounded as horrified as if Lexi had said she didn't know how to brush her teeth.

"Jesse makes doll clothes," Janet said. "She does it so good that people pay her. Like around Christmas? She made a mint."

"Someday maybe I'll have a doll hospital," Jesse said. When her muffin cheeks dimpled in a smile, she looked doll-like herself.

"Both my girls can do anything around the house," Aunt Jane said. "They get a lot of practice because I'm not much for domestic chores. I don't care for outside work, either. Some farm wife my poor Jake got." She laughed.

"Is that why you got rid of the animals?" Lexi asked.

"You were hoping for animals," Aunt Jane guessed. "Well, they're a lot of work. The one I mourn is our dog, Wolfie, and he died of old age. The only animals left around here are mice and spiders."

"And the boys," Janet said. "You always say they act like animals, Ma."

"Want to see my dolls?" Jesse asked. She had just finished a sandwich and a half.

"Sure," Lexi said.

She complimented Jesse extravagantly over the shelves

of dolls and baskets of meticulously hand sewn doll clothes in a hallway between the two huge attic bedrooms, one for the girls and one for the boys. Her enthusiasm seemed to please both her cousins.

"So," Janet said, "if you can learn to do an even running stitch, you can help us with the quilt. We promised to get it done by next month. They gave us the biggest part to do."

"I'd like to help," Lexi said. She hoped running stitches were easier than geometry quizzes. She also hoped they weren't planning to sew away the sunny hours of every day.

In the van on the way to the mall, Lexi asked Aunt Jane, "Did Jeb come in for lunch?"

"He'll eat when he's hungry. He's probably in the barn with his books."

"Books?" Lexi repeated in surprise. Aunt Jane seemed so unconcerned about Jeb.

"Jeb's the reader in the family. His nose is always in some book. It's either that or he's with his Indian friend."

The cousins snickered as if their mother had made a funny remark. Lexi said she didn't understand. Janet said, "It's this guy runs the convenience store. Trueblood. He claims to be half Indian and feeds Jeb all kinds of crazy tales."

"Jeb would have liked to've been an Indian," Aunt Jane said.

Funny, Lexi thought, she might have liked to have been one, too.

Inside the mall, Aunt Jane left them, telling them to meet her at the fountain in the center at four. Lexi trailed her cousins into a fabric store. They sauntered past standing bolts of cotton and rayon prints and solids to the back, where there were bins of remnants.

"Everyone's appliquéing a scene from the church calendar onto a square of plain white cloth, and then the quilting'll be like a frame around the picture squares," Janet explained. "We got to design our own squares. Can you draw?" she asked Lexi.

"Not me."

"Guess you do the designing then, Jesse," Janet said. "All I'm good for is plain sewing."

"What do you think of this for a border?" Jesse asked, holding up a cotton remnant with a small flowered pattern.

"Plain red or blue'd be better. Fit better with other people's squares," Janet said. "Don't you think?" She looked at Lexi.

"I don't know anything about making a quilt," Lexi admitted.

"What *do* you know?" Janet asked pleasantly. "What do you like to do?"

"Anything out-of-doors and I read a lot," Lexi admitted before she thought it through.

28

They gave her a double-barreled look. "I expect you're smart in school then. You went to a private school, didn't you?"

"Just this year. My parents sent me to boarding school because it was too dangerous where we were living. I didn't like Thistlewood Academy."

"Why not?"

"I didn't fit in there. They thought I was an oddball, I guess, because I don't care about clothes much and they did. . . . And they made up stories about me that weren't true."

They looked at her blank-faced and silent.

"They really did," Lexi said. The silence made her uneasy. It seemed like a chasm was opening between them, and she hurried to bridge it by saying, "I saw Jim giving Jeb a hard time this morning."

"Oh, yeah? What'd Jeb do now?" Janet asked.

"Something about losing Jim's ball." She thought telling his siblings should be okay.

"That Jeb. You'd think he'd learn, but he never does. If it isn't one thing it's another."

That wasn't the response Lexi had expected. "But Jim was mean," she explained. "I mean, Jeb didn't deserve to get beaten."

Jesse raised her eyebrows. "We don't tell on each other in this family."

"I'm just telling you," Lexi said. "I thought you might

know how to deal with Jim."

"He doesn't need dealing with," Jesse said. "Jeb's the one. Wait until you've been here awhile. You'll see."

They finally chose an assortment of solid-colored cotton remnants. "Time for refreshments," Janet said, and led the way through the mall to an ice cream store.

Lexi had a single dip. Her cousins both had doubles. "Our treat," Janet said when Lexi took out the change purse she'd brought along just in case.

"Oh, thank you," Lexi said.

"I guess you'd of had a double if you'd of thought we were treating," Jesse said.

It never would have occurred to her, but Lexi smiled rather than make an awkward denial.

"You watch your diet?" Jesse asked.

"No, I just don't gain weight," Lexi said.

"You ought to eat more. You could fit your whole self into one leg of Janet's jeans, you're so skinny," Jesse said.

Feeling like a toothpick, an unlovely one, Lexi followed them to the van. "So what'd you think of the mall?" Aunt Jane asked.

Lexi blinked. It had been a standard mall, a sprawling, one-story building with shops lined up on either side of an interior street, interrupted by a fountain in the center with benches nearby. A Sears was at one end and a discount store at the other. "It's okay," Lexi said.

"Okay?" Aunt Jane said. "Well, maybe you're used to

better, but we're real proud of our mall here. Before it went up a couple of years ago, we had a twenty-mile drive to town just to shop for a pair of sneakers."

"Sometimes we only come to walk around and have an ice cream," Jesse said.

"Umm," Lexi responded warily. That didn't sound like her idea of fun.

Jim and Joe were in the kitchen passing a half gallon milk container back and forth between them to wash down the enormous sandwiches they were eating.

"Where's your manners?" Aunt Jane said. "Can't you find any glasses?"

"Nope," Jim said. "You should have seen that homer I hit, Ma. It traveled clear across the county."

"Didn't you have any lunch?"

"Too busy."

Aunt Jane opened a cabinet and set a glass down beside him. "Well, it's time I started dinner. You'll have to eat again in an hour."

"No problem," Jim said.

"You seen Jeb?" she wanted to know.

"Not since this morning." Jim looked at Lexi as he asked his mother, "Want me to go see if he's in the barn?"

"Yes, tell him to come in now. Tell him I want him."

"May I go, too?" Lexi asked politely.

"Sure." Jim shrugged.

She followed him outside. There he turned and said, "Hey, I'm not mad at you, don't worry."

She frowned at him and said indignantly, "But I'm still mad at you for the way you beat up Jeb."

"What'd you do, come along to protect him from his bad big brother?"

"I just want to see how he is."

"You don't need to worry about Jeb. He can take it." Jim strode off ahead of her, broad shouldered and long legged. Handsome as he was, he didn't appeal to her. Bullies never had.

The barn was musty and dark, filled with awkward-looking machinery, old bottles, and cobwebs. A ladder led up to a loft half full of hay. Jim stood at the foot of the ladder and called, "Jeb, you up there? Ma wants you."

There were rustlings and then Jeb's head appeared. He climbed down the ladder slowly.

"You been up there the whole day?" Jim asked.

"I was reading," Jeb said quietly.

"Your cousin here was worrying I might still be mad at you. I'm not though."

"How come?"

"I found the ball. Dave gave it to me. You left it at the Indian's yesterday."

32

"Oh, good. I thought someone stole it," Jeb said. He smiled when Jim rested his arm across his shoulder. Jim looked at Lexi as if to say, see, he's not mad at me. She dropped her eyes. So far, in the matter of belonging to this family, her batting average was a big zero.

3

Lexi was anticipating the big family meal to come as she watched her aunt cutting up potatoes for the beef stew. But no sooner was the lid on the pot than Aunt Jane told her daughters, "There, now. That should be done by the time your dad gets home from work. You don't have to save none for me. I'll grab a hamburger at the bowling alley." A minute later she was out the door.

"Let's make a cake, seeing it's our cousin's first supper with us," Jesse said with enthusiasm.

"All right," Janet agreed. "We can try out that recipe the minister's wife gave us. You want to do the salad, Lexi?"

"Sure," she hastened to say, although she'd never put together a salad in her life. Cooking was another area her mother had posted Keep Out signs around. Still, she figured making a salad had to be simple. She found a head of lettuce and began slicing off small chunks.

"Hey!" Jesse yelped. "Aren't you going to wash it first?"

"Sorry." Lexi was embarrassed. Carefully, she rinsed off what she'd sliced, dumped it into a medium sized bowl, and began slicing the rest.

Jesse rolled her eyes. "You're supposed to tear it apart, not cut it with a knife."

Janet said patiently, "You need a bigger bowl, Lexi, and you better drain that water off or the lettuce'll be soggy."

"Don't you know how to cook, *either?*" Jesse asked.

"Well, I can boil water and toast bread," Lexi answered lightly.

"You're used to having servants wait on you, I bet," Jesse said. The way she said it was a put-down.

"No, I'm not. It's just that my mother never liked sharing the kitchen," Lexi said. "She taught me to play by myself and leave her alone."

"You're not close to your ma then?" Janet asked.

No, Lexi thought, she wasn't. But she was wary of admitting that painful truth in case her cousins might count it against her. Cautiously she said, "My mother's a very private person. She keeps to herself. Dad's the one

I talk to most. Trouble is he works sixteen-hour days, so he's not around much." Their expressions were neutral as they listened to her. Lexi expanded on her explanation.

"See, Dad's responsible for bringing these big construction jobs in on time and on budget, and things are always going wrong. Like materials don't get delivered or the workers suddenly take a holiday or . . ." She took a breath. Now they were looking at her as if she were speaking a foreign language. Her heart squeezed. Was she doing it again, making herself strange to them when all she meant to do was help them to understand her? What was wrong with her that even her own cousins found her strange?

To change the subject, she asked, "Umm—is this bowl okay?"

It was. "What should I put in the salad besides lettuce?" she asked, to be sure she made no more mistakes.

Jesse's big caramel-colored eyes rolled as if the question was stupid beyond belief. Janet said, "Why don't you just help clean up after, and we'll do the meal."

"Cleanup's the boys' job," Jesse said. "Jeb usually does it 'cause Jim and Joe are never around."

"Well, I could set the table," Lexi offered.

"No need," Janet said. "What we do is leave the food on the counter and everyone grabs a plate and helps themselves when they want."

"And Jim and Joe don't have to do anything?" Lexi asked. That sounded unfair to her.

"They do garbage and outside work—when you can catch them long enough to make them," Janet said.

Apparently the family also ate *where* they wanted. While Jesse was making frosting for the cake, Lexi discovered Jim and Joe eating their stew in the living room in front of the TV. So much for the big, happy family meals she had imagined. That Christmas dinner must have been unique for them, too.

Jeb appeared, book in hand. He pulled a stool next to the kitchen counter, spooned some stew and salad onto a plate and propped the book open so that he could read and eat at the same time.

Lexi took some salad and a small portion of potatoes and carrots from the stew. She was a vegetarian by preference. She sat down at the big table next to Janet, who was methodically chewing her way through her dinner. Jesse had wandered off to the living room with her heaped plate. Lexi toyed with her food, wistfully remembering a goat stew she had shared with Ezekiel's family. They had sat around a fire in a tight, warm circle, talking softly in the night. They'd offered her the choicest tidbits, listened to her, laughed with her. The warm currents of their affection for one another lapped around her, and poor as they seemed, she had envied them.

Jesse came back to eat her share of the fluffy, frosted,

coconut-lemon layer cake. "Isn't it awesome?" Jesse asked Lexi. "Our minister's wife won a prize for it at the county fair last summer."

"Umm," Lexi murmured. Seeing Janet eyeing the small piece she was toying with, Lexi forced herself to put another forkful of too-sweet cake in her mouth.

"Lexi's probably used to fancy desserts with rum and cream," Jesse said. Her eyes, too, were fixed disapprovingly on Lexi's plate.

"Oh, no. At school they mostly served puddings, and my mother doesn't bake," Lexi hastened to say. "Well, she's never had an oven she can trust. Most places we've lived you don't get a power supply for more than a couple of hours a day."

Again their blank looks silenced her. Either she was boring them or they just couldn't imagine a life so different from their own.

"I guess you had fun, though," Janet said doubtfully.

Lexi nodded. Her fun had consisted of walks with Ezekiel to see the sun set through the twisted branches of the baobab tree and observe the few remaining wild animals that came to the water hole to drink. She was saved from confessing that when Jesse asked, "Can you sing? We could use another soprano in the church choir."

"I'm not much of a singer," Lexi admitted. Silence. She could see their eyes wondering what she *was* good at.

Bravely she continued, "But I'm a pretty decent fisher-man." She smiled.

Janet snorted. "You and Jeb. When he's not up in the barn reading, he's out on the riverbank. Then if he catches a fish, like as not, he throws it back. It's no wonder he gets picked on in school when he acts so weird." She was looking over her shoulder at Jeb as she spoke. He ignored her, set his empty plate in the sink, and walked out of the kitchen.

"They don't pick on him so much anymore, Janet," Jesse said after Jeb left. "Not since Jim taught him how to fight."

"Jim taught him, but *does* Jeb fight back?"

"Well, I don't know, but I heard he butted a kid in the belly and knocked the wind out of him."

Janet laughed. "Little goat. That ought to be his Indian name."

Later, when the kitchen table had been taken over by the quilting project, Jeb returned to do the dishes. Lexi gave up trying to make stitches even enough to satisfy Jesse, put her scrap of practice material aside, and got up to help Jeb. She heard Jesse whispering frantically to Janet. "You *can't* let her work on the quilt. She'll ruin it."

"Well, she could cut out some squares for us," Janet said. More loudly, she asked Lexi, "You can cut straight, can't you?"

Suddenly Lexi got angry. They were making her feel like an all-around failure, and she wasn't. At least, no one had ever made her feel that way before. Pretending she hadn't heard Janet, she began stacking dirty dishes on the counter next to the sink. Saying nothing was safer than spitting out something sharp that would make her cousins give up on her altogether. Truthfully, by Janet and Jesse's standards, she was a failure. No matter that her father had called her his tough little sprout. What he gave her credit for was adjusting rapidly to so many surroundings, from tropical islands and dismal backwaters of the Amazon, to the Arizona desert in 115-degree summer heat, to drought and poverty-stricken surroundings in Africa, to eccentric adult companions and children whose language was foreign to her. She could speak common words in five different languages and knew what to do for snake bite and bee sting. And she was as good a fisherman as her father. Take it easy, she told herself. You'll learn the language here, too. It's always hard at first in a new place. Except here, she had expected it to be easy.

Uncle Jake came through the kitchen door. Without greeting anyone, he began silently loading a plate with food for himself.

"You have a good day, Papa?" Janet asked him.

"Same as usual," he said. Then he nodded at Lexi and

proceeded to the living room to eat his meal in front of the TV set.

Janet and Jesse packed up the graph paper on which they were trying to design their quilting sections and followed him to the TV.

Jeb was scraping dishes into the garbage pail. "I can do that," Lexi said. He let her.

"You want to wash or dry?" he asked, taking her dishwashing ability for granted.

"Don't you have a dishwasher?"

"Yeah, but it's full. I forgot to run it after breakfast."

"I'll wash." She found the detergent and a stopper for the sink, cleared dirty dishes out of it and began. He leaned his elbows on the counter and watched her without comment, a dish towel hanging from his pocket. She washed and rinsed under the running water and handed him the first dish. Then she realized the sink would soon be full and she'd have to somehow let some water out. Even dishwashing was defeating her. To hide her dismay, she asked him, "So what kind of books do you read?"

"Any kind, but I like to read about Indians best. I got this book, *The Light in the Forest,* it's about a boy like me that gets raised by Indians, and he'd rather be an Indian. He sees how they're better."

"Better than who?"

"Than the white man. 'Cause Indians respect the land. And they don't believe anybody owns it, and they're brave and free."

"Not too many Indians left, though," she pointed out gently.

"Well, there's some. Even around here. Trueblood seen signs in the mountains."

"Really? Are they the same kind of Indian Trueblood is?"

"Well, not exactly. See, he's only part Indian and he wasn't raised to live in the woods. He says he'd rather take his chances with the white man and drive his camper down to Florida winters." Jeb shrugged.

"What's Trueblood's tribe?"

"He's part Onondaga. The Onondagas were big guns in the Iroquois confederation. You know Hiawatha?"

She nodded. "I've read about him."

"Well, he was an Onondaga. Or maybe he was a Mohawk. Anyway, he was the one got the other tribes to agree to join together. And they made a constitution that was even better than ours. They were really smart, those Iroquois."

"I'd like to read the book after you're done with it," she said.

"Sure." He sounded pleased. "I could introduce you to Trueblood, too, if you want."

"Would you? I'd like that," she said.

"We could go now. Want to?"

"Tonight?" She wasn't eager to meet anyone new after all the day's disappointments.

"It's only about a quarter of a mile. He runs the convenience store. You're not afraid of the dark, are you?"

"No, but why not wait until tomorrow?"

"Well, nights he's not so busy," Jeb said. "During the day, people stop for gas, and he's got to go out to the pump, and they want cigarettes or ice cream or something."

"Okay, but I'm going to be here for the whole summer," she said.

"Well, I'm not."

"No? Where are you going?"

"Somewhere," he said mysteriously.

"Is it a secret?" He didn't answer, but she read his thoughts as if they were printed on his sensitive face. He was going to look for those Indians in the hills. Were there really any there? She doubted it. But suppose, just suppose there were. What a thrill it would be to find them!

"Tomorrow," she told him. "I'd like to go with you tomorrow, Jeb."

He looked at her. Although she couldn't tell which eye was doing the looking, she could tell he was earnestly considering her. "Okay," he said finally. "Trueblood might like you. He don't like my sisters. He says they're white squaws, but you maybe. He might like you."

It cheered her up immediately that Jeb thought his Indian friend might like her. It gave her hope that she wasn't a total misfit after all.

4

exi called a good-night to the silent group of television watchers and went upstairs to write a letter to her parents.

"The big news from my first day here," she wrote, "is *I* made the salad for dinner. Aren't you amazed, Mom? Also Janet and Jesse are teaching me to sew. Cooking, sewing, and eating are their things. The weather's beautiful but they don't seem to care about the out-of-doors. Of the boy cousins, Jeb's my favorite so far. He's the one my age and he's a reader. *His* big thing is Indians. Considering how my cousins are, don't be surprised if I turn up fat, pale, and in feathers next time you see me."

She maintained the jolly tone while reporting about her aunt's job and new hairdo. As for her uncle, she said, "the most I can say about Uncle Jake is he doesn't waste words."

It sounded reasonably upbeat, she decided on rereading the letter, and upbeat was what she wanted for her father. He had enough to worry about without her whining that she feared she'd made a mistake coming here.

"You sure go to bed early," Janet commented. She had returned from the bathroom in striped men's pajamas. Jesse was undressing with her back toward Lexi. For a wonder she didn't put on striped pajamas, too, but a dainty, flowered cotton nightgown.

Outside a loud symphony of peeping frogs and *shushing* wind was playing. Lexi lay with her hands clasped behind her head, hoping the darkness would invite her cousins' confidences. But Janet mumbled, "Good night," and Jesse yawned and said, "Night," and then there was silence. Before long one of them began a soft snoring. They're asleep, just like that, Lexi told herself in amazement. Sleep rarely came easily to her. She lay still, listening to the night music. It wasn't the chatter of female cousins, but it reminded her a little of home.

What had Ezekiel taught her, he of the high cheekbones and gentle eyes? "Man is at one with the creatures of the earth. We are all one single, breathing body. We can never be lonely." But she didn't feel a part of any-

46

thing here, and Ezekiel was dead. "Ezekiel," she whispered longingly into the dark. "Ezekiel, my friend."

When she woke up the next morning, the room was empty. It was almost ten o'clock. They must think she was a real slugabed. No note left for her in the kitchen this time. She got herself some cereal and ate it, thinking she would go exploring outside for fun. A noise behind her made her jump. It was Joe.

"Hi," she said cheerfully. "What are you up to?"

"Nothing," he mumbled. He ducked his head and scooted past her to the bathroom. He was in there a long time. When he came out, he blushed and hurried out the back door. Boy, was he a shy one, as silent as his father, Lexi thought.

Looking through the screen door, she saw him join Jim, who was hoeing weeds in a vegetable garden. Now *that* she could do. Except she didn't want to do anything with Jim, not after the way he'd beaten Jeb. Beyond the vegetable garden was a row of trees and somewhere around here was a river. Nobody was likely to shoot at her or kidnap her here, in this quiet countryside in the Catskill mountains of upstate New York. She would go find the river.

On her way past the barn, she heard a thunk. She stopped beside wide-open doors to listen. The smell of old hay, leather, and animal droppings lured her in. Another thunk. The third one came as she climbed the ladder to the loft. Jeb was shooting arrows across the width of the barn loft into a target made of bound-together straw. Three arrows stuck out of the wheel-sized target.

"I guess you *would* make a good Indian," she said.

"Yeah, I'm practicing. Because they can't use guns up there or people will hear them. Trueblood says a brave's got to be able to bring food back to the tribe."

"And what does an Indian girl get to do? Rock the baby?"

"I don't know. Maybe . . . You want to try this bow? Trueblood lent it to me. I got to return it today."

She stood sideways and held the bow at arm's length straight in front of her with her fist at eye level, as he directed her, and gained a healthy respect for his strength. The bow was heavy and the string too tightly strung for her to pull. Even the steel-tipped arrow seemed heavy and dangerous. "Bet you could scare a rabbit to death with this just by aiming it," she said.

He laughed. "You want to come with me to True-blood's now?"

"Sure." She'd go exploring later, and perhaps he'd go with her.

He slid the bow and arrows into a burlap bag. "So that my brothers won't see what I've got," Jeb explained. "Trueblood said not to let anyone else touch it."

But Jeb had let her touch it, Lexi was pleased to note.

48

No one was around. She'd been trained to leave word about where she was off to whenever she left the house. Here, it seemed adults didn't worry about kids' whereabouts. This peaceful, green, growing world must be really safe.

A row of shaggy-headed trees grew on their side of the road, and on the other side was a fenced-in pasture with holsteins, white cows with black spots. They looked up, still chewing their cuds, and watched Lexi and Jeb walk by their quarter of a mile of lumpy pasture. It was speckled with gray rocks, mudholes, flowering weeds, and an occasional broad-armed tree. Woods had overgrown the fields on the other side of the road.

"It's pretty around here," Lexi said. "But where's the river?"

"You haven't seen the river yet? It's back of the house right behind the trees." He pointed.

"You fish there?"

"Yeah."

"I love fishing," Lexi said.

He looked at her and grinned. In profile, when you couldn't see how mismatched his eyes were, he was actually cute looking, not handsome like Jim, but definitely cute. She wondered if being cross-eyed bothered him. No doubt it would, she thought, because it would make him seem different from other kids and that meant trouble. "Do kids around here tease a lot?" she asked him.

49

"Yeah," he said. "Anyways, they tease me a lot."

"About what?"

"About not knowing what's going on because I'm too busy reading, and because I like Indians."

Not his eyes then. "So what do they do to you?" she asked.

"Stick out their feet so I'll stumble, dump my books in the mud, call me names like redskin."

"You mean your brothers?"

"No, in school. Mostly I don't get in trouble at home because I keep out of the way."

She thought of the beating he'd taken. Didn't he consider that getting in trouble? "But if you told your parents, wouldn't they do something?" Lexi asked.

"What?" He looked at her questioningly. "Mom says what's between kids you got to handle yourself. If I got in trouble with a teacher, she'd come to school, but I'm quiet so teachers don't mind me."

They turned onto a paved road and came to a crossroads. The store was a small, weathered, gray building behind two gas pumps. Inside, it was crowded with double-sided shelves that held bread and hair tonic and toothpaste, cans of soup and bags of potato chips, a whole row of cookies. A glass-topped freezer stocked with ice cream and bags of ice cubes stood beside a tall, glass-doored refrigerator full of beer and soda.

The only unusual objects were on a shelf in back of the cash register and counter. There Lexi saw a lineup of worn-looking Indian artifacts: a peace pipe, a beaded leather pouch, some crude pots and baskets.

Jeb saw her looking. "That stuff's for real. Trueblood traded with Indians for it."

"The ones hiding in the woods?" Lexi asked. "But what would they need? I thought they were self-sufficient."

"Who's this girl?" a harsh voice asked. Lexi saw a tall man with high cheekbones and prominent brows that hid his eyes coming down the aisle toward them. He had jet black hair in a braid down his back and a band with a feather in it around his forehead. His left cheek was badly scarred.

"She's my cousin. Come to spend the summer with us," Jeb said quickly. And then proudly he introduced her. "Lexi, this is my friend, Trueblood."

Trueblood growled like a guard dog, deep in his throat. "What did you tell her?"

"Just what you said . . . she won't tell anyone, Trueblood. She's okay."

"How do you know?" Trueblood asked.

"Lexi," Jeb said pleadingly, "you wouldn't give them away, would you?"

Something about the man's deliberate menace made her want to stand up to him. "I don't believe there could be any Indians hiding out in the woods," she said. "After all we're only a hundred and twenty or thirty miles from New York City. Where could they hide?"

"Now there's your typical woman, Jeb," Trueblood said mockingly. "Can't fool her with any stories. She knows what's real and what ain't. Without even knowing she knows."

"But you said—you told me you were sure," Jeb protested. "You said you could even tell me how to get there."

"Lies," Trueblood said. "I was just feeding you lies."

"Then where'd you get the basket and that pipe. Didn't you trade for them?" Jeb asked.

"The Indian I traded with was just a boy. Who knows where he come from?"

"What did you give him?" Lexi asked curiously. "I mean in exchange?"

"Gifts for his grandfather. Aspirin and chewing gum to make the old man want to live, but he died anyhow and the boy left his tribe. Went up north to Canada. . . . What do you care about Indians?" he asked Lexi suddenly.

"They're different," she said, "and so am I."

"You? You're white and female. You got a mama to care for you," Trueblood said.

"My mother's in Africa," Lexi said. "And even if she were here, she doesn't care about me. She didn't want a child."

"Is that so?" Trueblood looked as if he was considering. Then he thundered, "The white man stole the Indians' land and broke their spirit. What you read now about the environment and how we got to live in harmony with nature? The Indian knew that a thousand years ago. He knew. But the white man polluted the earth and now he's got to suffer for what he done."

"It looks as if there's a lot of nature left around here," Lexi said.

Trueblood drew himself up tall and took a deep breath. "Some, yeah. There's nights when the Milky Way is so bright you can imagine . . . maybe."

For a while the three of them were silent. Then Jeb said, "I brought back your bow, and I didn't lose any arrows, Trueblood. Not one."

"Did you practice?"

Jeb nodded. "I guess I could shoot a rabbit if I had to."

Trueblood grinned a lopsided grin that showed bad teeth. "Bet you couldn't. Bet you'd starve in the woods without a bag of cookies along."

"Lexi likes to fish," Jeb said.

"Is that so?" Trueblood leaned on the counter next to the cash register.

"She's not like my sisters."

"Where do you come from?" Trueblood asked her.

"Africa," she boasted a little to impress him. "And I've lived in the Amazon and in the desert in Arizona."

"No kidding. Making it on your own with just a fish-line and a piece of string?" He was mocking her again.

"No, but—"

"You sleep in a nice cozy bed and get three meals a day put on the table for you, right?" he asked.

"Yes," she admitted.

"Well, the Indians don't. They eat one meal a day mostly and practice going hungry for when there's nothing. They concentrate on staying alive. You ever do that?"

"I've never had to," she said.

"No, I wouldn't think so," Trueblood said.

"Have you?" she asked him boldly.

He smiled. He looked evil when that left side of his mouth lifted into the scarred cheek. "Well," he said, contemplating her. "Well, well, well." He took a dirty-looking, flat basket from the shelf behind the cash register and offered it to her. She held it in both hands. It was roughly woven with spaces between the reeds.

"That basket was held by a squaw a thousand years ago," Trueblood intoned. "In it she sifted the cornmeal she'd ground. All day she had to pound that corn with a big rock tied to a stick. Hour after hour she pounded those hard little kernels."

His voice brought the Indian woman to life so that Lexi could hear the monotonous thud of the stone tool and feel the ache in her upper arms from lifting it. She turned the basket over in her hands to examine it rather

54

than be mesmerized by his eyes as well as his voice. *China,* the tiny red letters spelled out. China! She kept her eyes on the basket, embarrassed at catching him out in a lie.

He chuckled and said, "Now you don't believe me, do you?"

"Not about this." She handed the basket made in China back to him.

"Well, you're right. This here's not Indian made. It's *like* what they used, though. . . . You got a smart cousin here, Jeb."

"Well," Jeb said bluntly, "she can't sew or cook or pull the bow hard enough to shoot it."

"Maybe what else she's got in her head is better. The Iroquois made the smart old grandma their leader. She was the one chose the next chief. Iroquois women ran the camp while the men were out hunting. They planted and fished and made the clothes—everything they needed to live. What's more, they worked in a group. They knew how to share with one another. That's why they couldn't get along with the white man. The Indians shared everything, but the white man's greedy. He wants to own everything himself."

"But you own things, don't you?" Lexi asked, looking around the store.

"This place? I inherited it from my cousin. Old man died and left me his place and his camper. So I come

55

here. It's as good a spot as any for a man alone like me."

"Did your family teach you about Indians?" she asked.

"No. My mama was Indian, but she died when I was small. Then I was a foster child, lived around in white man's houses. What I learned about Indians come from books."

"Did you fool me, Trueblood? Was it all lies?" Jeb sounded shaky.

"No," Trueblood said. "Everything I told you, everything is the god's honest truth."

Jeb gulped and looked at his friend trustingly.

"Now what do you say to that, girl?" Trueblood asked Lexi.

"Would you show us?" she asked. "I mean, if there really are Indians and you've seen signs."

"Why should I?"

"Please, Trueblood, you promised," Jeb pleaded.

"She going with you?"

They both looked at Lexi.

"Maybe, I might go," she said, and her heartbeat picked up speed. Adventure. Nearly as strong as her yearning to belong was her itch for adventure.

"We'll see." Trueblood said.

"Tell her the story of the lost boy, Trueblood," Jeb urged then. "Please."

"Why do you like that story so much? You tell it to her. You know it by heart," Trueblood said. A horn honked outside. "Customer," Trueblood muttered, and he loped out the door to the gas pump.

"Do you like him?" Jeb asked.

"Well, I don't know how much of his stories to believe."

"I believe him. He's my friend," Jeb said proudly.

Trueblood had returned to make change. He'd heard what Lexi had said. He punched open the cash register and said, "True stories are the only ones worth telling."

"But you told Jeb there's a secret tribe of Indians living up in the hills. That can't be true, can it?" she asked him.

"Maybe not a tribe, but what's left of one."

"You'll take us there, won't you?" Jeb begged.

"I told you. You got to find them yourself. They wouldn't appreciate me turning them into a tourist attraction."

Trueblood finished with his customer and asked, "You kids got any money to spend?"

"No," Jeb said. "I just came to return your bows and arrows."

"Okay then, on your way. I'm busy," Trueblood said.

"Oh." Jeb sounded disappointed. "Well, can I come by tomorrow?"

"I'll be here," Trueblood said.

"And can Lexi come, too?"

"If she wants." Trueblood's crooked smile put her off again. Her father had taught her to judge people by their acts, not their looks, Lexi chided herself. Besides, Jeb liked Trueblood, and she trusted Jeb.

As they approached the farm, Lexi asked Jeb to point the way to the river. "Come on. I'll show you," he said.

5

The river was just a little too wide to throw a stone across and shadowed by the trees and brush on its banks. Where rocks and dead tree trunks broke the smooth flow, the water was rumpled. "Can you swim in this?" Lexi asked Jeb.

"Up by the bend near town is where kids swim. There's a bridge my brothers jump from there, but the water's still kind of cold."

"You don't jump from the bridge?" Lexi asked.

"I'm not much of a swimmer."

"What about Janet and Jesse?"

"All's they ever do is wade on a real hot day. They don't do much outdoors unless it's a church picnic."

"I like to swim," Lexi said. She recalled how Ezekiel had clapped his hands and praised her when she showed him how she could. Even though he was a man, he hadn't known how to swim. She had promised to teach him—someday, on one of the somedays he never had.

Across the river, odd, feathery evergreens screened the hillside, filtering sunlight through their branches. The brown, needle-covered ground beneath them looked inviting. Downriver Lexi saw a green, furred mountain hump carrying a wreath of white clouds. "Do you ever go camping or hiking around here, Jeb?" she asked.

"No. Hunters'll go in the woods, but it's pretty wild. Once you get back a ways it's easy to get lost. Unless you're an Indian."

She could imagine a muscular bronze Indian brave with a single feather in his hair skulking through the clearings. What was harder was to believe a bunch of Indians could hide out somewhere in this peaceful landscape. "Did Trueblood give you an idea of where those Indians live?"

"He can't. He took an oath. Even under torture, he can't tell."

"Who's going to torture him?"

Jeb shrugged. "The white man I guess."

"Oh, come on!" Lexi said. "Can you see your dad torturing Trueblood to find out where some Indians are hiding?"

"Well, but why are there so few left? If the white man had treated them fair all along, there'd be plenty of them around. Right? Like when the colonists first came to this country. They wouldn't of survived if the Indians hadn't showed them how to grow corn and stuff. You learn that in school even. Right?"

"I guess it's possible there are some in the woods," Lexi said. "Anything's possible."

"Right. And I'm going to look for them," Jeb said. "Trueblood says Indians adopt kids, even white kids."

"Really? You want to get adopted?"

"Maybe. . . . You won't tell my family, will you?"

"Of course not," she assured him. "But why, Jeb?"

"Because . . . nothing I do's any good here, but with them I might do good." He considered her silently for a minute and then he confided, "I'm building myself a raft. I started it in the barn. Soon's I get some long pieces of lumber, I'll be done. Then I'm going that way." He pointed toward the mountains. "When I find the right place, I'll beach the raft and start searching for them."

"The right place?" she questioned.

Jeb nodded. "Trueblood says when I'm ready he'll tell me what to look for."

A scent of pine wafted past Lexi on a fresh breeze. She sniffed deep, staring at a white V of wake the river was making around a tree branch. The current must be faster than it seemed. She liked being here much better than being an apprentice seamstress in the house with Janet and Jesse. Impulsively, she asked, "Can I help you with the raft, Jeb?"

He smiled. His bony face looked sweet when the tightness left it. "Not much left to do, but you can see it. Come to the barn this afternoon. Don't say a word to the girls, though."

"Don't worry. I won't."

He started walking away from the river, but he turned back to say, "I never thought I'd have a friend that was a girl. I like you, Lexi."

She was too touched to speak. Well, she liked him, too.

An hour later, she had found a good spot along the riverbank to fish from, but the sky had darkened suddenly and it began to rain hard. She ran back to the house. Jeb had disappeared—into the barn no doubt. The lighted kitchen invited her indoors. She joined Janet and Jesse at the kitchen table where they were, as she'd expected, working on their quilting.

"Where'd you go this morning?" Janet wanted to know.

"Jeb was showing me around."

"Jeb, huh? He introduce you to his friend?" Janet's smile was just a glint in her eyes.

"Trueblood? Yes, I met him."

"Nobody likes him much around here. He goes to the tavern after the store closes Saturday nights," Jesse said.

"Well, I guess he needs some entertainment," Lexi said. While she hadn't liked Trueblood particularly, she had the urge to defend him for Jeb's sake.

"He's new around here. He only came when his cousin died and he inherited the store," Jesse said.

"I know," Lexi said.

"Well, nobody knows where he comes from or much about him," Jesse said. "He could be a jailbird for all we know. He looks like a jailbird."

"So far we don't know anything bad about him, Jesse," Janet said.

"Well, he looks evil," Jesse insisted.

"He can't help his looks," Janet said. "And the store's a lot cleaner since he took it over. His stuff is fresher. Used to be everything was flyspecked and stale. Now it's okay."

"Anyway, I think Jeb picks weird friends," Jesse said.

Lexi asked Janet, who was obviously the fairer-minded sister, how long Trueblood had lived there. Two, three years was the answer.

"And Jeb's his only friend?"

"I can't say," Janet said. "He might have drinking buddies in the tavern. Nobody from our church knows him. He never goes to church."

"You want to help with this quilt now?" Jesse asked her.

"Sure," Lexi said.

"Well, you could start cutting out shapes by this pattern, but you got to be really careful. Cut crooked and your pieces won't sew up right."

Lexi nodded. She'd cut out enough paper dolls in her life to be confident she could cut straight. With scissors, fabric, and a simple pattern in hand, she asked Jesse how many they needed.

"Lots. Get as many as you can out of the material," Jesse said.

Four eyes watched Lexi pin the pattern on. Four eyes watched her cut. The time she'd dried her mother's crystal goblets after a party flashed in her mind. But as she began cutting her second piece, her cousins returned their attention to their design work. Apparently, she'd passed the test.

Quietly the sisters began to argue with each other about how to do the wedding scene on the square which was to be the center of their part of the quilt. The quilt would picture scenes from church life. Janet wanted to show the back of the bride and groom and the head of the minister blessing them. Jesse wanted to do a frontal view of the bride and groom walking out the church door. Lexi's little shapes were for the borders framing the scene. She was cutting out her sixth one when Jesse gasped. "Lexi, what are you doing?"

"Huh?" Lexi froze in mid scissor cut.

"You're not cutting on the straight of the fabric."

"I'm not?" Lexi looked in guilty confusion at the material she'd been cutting. What had she done wrong?

"See," Jesse pulled a thread to show her that the material had been cut at a slant, and by following the cut edge, Lexi wasn't cutting her pieces straight across.

"But what difference does it make?" Lexi asked.

"What difference?" Jesse screeched.

"Jesse, simmer down," Janet ordered her sister. "There's still enough material left to get what we need. I hope." To Lexi, she said comfortingly, "It's okay. We should've watched you. You just never learned to sew."

Neither Jesse's red-faced spluttering nor Janet's forgiveness eased Lexi's embarrassment. "I think I'll go read," she murmured.

"You do that," Janet agreed.

Lexi slunk off to the bedroom. She got out *The Fellowship of the Ring,* which she'd brought along to reread, and retreated to Tolkien country.

A couple of hours later she stood up and stretched. The rain had stopped its soft-shoe dance on the roof. She thought she'd go out to the barn and see what Jeb was doing.

"Hi," she called, stepping into the shadowed hollow where he was pounding away at something.

Jeb jumped. He was nailing wood strips to a square framework. "Oh, it's you," he said, hammer suspended in air. "Could you hear me outside?"

"Yes, but your sisters are in the house, and nobody else's around."

"Good. What time is it?"

"Around three, I guess."

"Jim and Joe could come back. I better stop in case they get home early."

"Why?" She was mystified. "Oh, you mean they wouldn't want you going out on the river?"

"No. It don't matter to them if I drown, but they can't know about this raft. Don't tell them, Lexi."

"I won't." She guessed he was afraid they would mock him. The raft did look primitive, just a few boards laid crosswise across a row of closely spaced wood strips. "Do you think that's going to float?"

"Wood floats, yeah. Besides, I'm going to shellac it so it won't get waterlogged. Paddles is the problem. I got to figure out some way to get some. Otherwise it might get hung up on rocks or something."

Remembering the sewing fiasco, she decided not to offer to hammer any nails in for him. "Want me to keep watch for your brothers?"

"Would you? Boy, that'd be a big help. They'll be com-

66

ing up the road past Trueblood's store. Soon as you spot them, run back here and warn me, okay?"

"Okay," she agreed cheerfully. Being a lookout was a boring job, but at least it was one she could do. She walked out to the road and found a tree with a conveniently low branch. Tree climbing was one of her skills. It wouldn't win her any points from Janet and Jesse, though. She perched on the branch and swung her legs as she watched the dirt road. Other than small brown birds in the bushes and a truck that rattled by, there wasn't much happening.

If an Indian tribe were managing to hide out in the woods around here, they couldn't find her any more useless than her cousins were finding her, she thought. What if the Indians were willing to adopt her? She loved being out-of-doors. Maybe she was meant to be an Indian. Maybe it was her fate. She imagined herself grinding corn and humming to quiet the papoose hanging snug in its cradleboard from the branch nearby. The worn face of the Indian mother would smile on her efforts. The breeze would cool her. . . .

When the squalling began, she jumped from her lookout seat and raced to the barn. Two bikes were leaning against the faded red siding. Somehow Jim and Joe had gotten past her. They must have come from an unexpected direction. Judging by the fury in Jim's voice, Jeb was in trouble again.

"My wood. You knew that was my wood. I traded my whole collection of baseball cards for it, and you went and just took it."

"I didn't know," Jeb squealed. "I didn't know it was yours. I just found it by the old chicken house."

"It was for a duck blind we were going to build," Joe said. "Jim and me were going to build a duck blind, and now you got it all messed up."

"How are you going to pay for this?" Jim said, shaking Jeb roughly. "You going to get me back my baseball cards?"

"I'll pay for it," Lexi said. They turned and looked at her. "How much does it cost?"

"That's maybe twenty, thirty dollars worth of wood he took," Jim said, snaking his eyes at her.

"It is not," Jeb said.

"I'll give you fifteen," Lexi said.

Jim snorted. "Guess you got a rich friend, Jeb." He released Jeb, who slumped and rubbed his right shoulder. "Well, okay," Jim said to her. "Let's see the money." It was a challenge.

"I'll get it." She marched upstairs to her suitcase. She hadn't wanted to take the spending money. Her father had insisted. "You might need it. There might be an emergency," he had said. Well, this was an emergency, although not the kind he'd expected. Was she being foolish to bail Jeb out? The way things were going, she might need her cash for a bus ticket out of here. She took out a ten and a five from the cache of bills in the zippered pocket of her jean jacket.

It was only after she'd paid off Jim that she wondered if the reason Jeb had been so worried about being found out by his brothers was because he had known the wood he was using was Jim's. That would make cousin Jeb a little crooked. And Trueblood? He didn't look very reliable. Suppose she'd chosen the wrong people to fit in with in this serene countryside. Still, of them all, she liked Jeb best.

6

Jeb thought Trueblood might know where to get the paddles they needed. "But it's almost dinnertime, isn't it? We can't just take off," Lexi said.

"They won't care, and they'll save us something to eat. Don't worry."

Missing a meal didn't worry her. Visiting Trueblood again did. Something about him made her hackles rise, but Jeb was so eager that she went.

Trueblood was sitting outside the entrance to his store whittling in the dusk.

"Turtle?" Jeb asked when he saw the crude, hand-sized wooden figure up close.

"Yep," Trueblood said. "This'll hang by my door. Any clansmen of mine come by here, they'll see I'm one of them."

"I didn't know you were Turtle Clan." Jeb sounded disappointed.

Trueblood grinned his lopsided grin. "What'd you expect? Wolf? Or a bear maybe?"

"Yeah," Jeb admitted.

"That's because you don't know anything," Trueblood said. "Back before the white man took and ruined everything, turtle was the most powerful clan." He held the carving out in the palm of his hand for them to see. The roughly shaped shell had no feet; its snaky head looked too small for its body.

"Why do you live here where there aren't any Indians around except you?" Lexi asked.

"This was all Indian hunting grounds, everything around here," Trueblood said. "Every rock, every tree holds the spirit of my people."

"But don't you get lonely?" Lexi asked. "I mean for somebody live?"

"I don't need no one," Trueblood said.

"You said there was live Indians left in the woods," Jeb blurted out. "That's what you told me, Trueblood. You said I could find them if I looked hard enough."

Trueblood's narrow gaze shifted to Lexi, but he spoke harshly to Jeb. "No Indian boy'd ever give up his secret

71

to the enemy. They could rip his nails out, bite off the ends of his fingers, burn him, and he'd never tell. He'd sing his war song in their faces while they were killing him."

"But she's going with me," Jeb pleaded. "My cousin and me, we're going to find them and get them to adopt us."

"Is that so?" Trueblood's eyes glinted. His teeth showed as the right side of his lip lifted. "So you want to be an Indian, too? I took you for a city girl."

"I don't know if I want to be an Indian," Lexi said carefully. "But I haven't found where I belong. It might be with them."

His face relaxed and he studied her in silence. With the usual mockery gone from his eyes, she felt more at ease with him, and she asked, "Are you really sure there are Indians out there? Have you met them?"

"I've seen their signs," Trueblood said earnestly. "But I never met them except in dreams."

"Well, what are the signs? What do we look for?" she asked.

"You might better ask me about the dreams. An Indian finds his truth in dreams. . . . Take how a boy becomes a man. The boy goes off in the woods alone to fast and suffer until he dreams his guardian spirit. Only when he gets his guardian spirit can he return to his people. You want to be an Indian, learn to dream first."

"But I'm not a boy," Lexi said. "What about girls?"

He chuckled and teased, "Well, to my mind a girl's nothing but a worthless creature. But those old Iroquois, their women owned everything. Everything. Not land. Indians didn't own the land. That belongs to the Great Spirit. It can only be used and has to be treated right. But what they made themselves—the skin clothing decorated with porcupine quills and vegetable dyes, the longhouse where the clan lived in like apartments, the baskets and tools and sacred things for ceremonies, the winter furs and wampum—all that the women owned."

"So what did the men have?" Lexi asked.

"Well, a man married into his wife's wealth. She didn't get from him. He got what she had, and he went to her longhouse and joined her family and left his own. Those Iroquois women, they had power."

"I thought the longhouses were up north," Lexi said.

"Where did you learn that?" Trueblood demanded.

"I read it somewhere. I read a lot."

"That so? Well, what you get from books won't help you much in the woods, girl." His voice had regained its edge.

Jeb put in, "Lexi paid Jim for the wood I made the raft with."

"Did she?"

"Now all's I need is paddles."

"Paddles, eh?" Trueblood's lip went up at one corner.

He squinted at Lexi. "How much cash you got for a pair?"

"How much do they cost?" she asked.

He thought. "Well, seeing as it's for a friend, five dollars might do it."

"Okay," Lexi agreed.

He took them to a shed behind the store. Lexi saw shelves of dirty bottles and jugs, plastic and glass, chains, twists of rope, broken tools, engine parts, and indeed a pair of scarred and weathered paddles. Trueblood presented them to Jeb with a flourish. "There you go."

"Awesome," Jeb said. He turned to Lexi. "Okay?"

She nodded. "But I don't have the money with me."

"You can bring it later," Trueblood said. And he added pointedly, "See, I trust *you.*"

"You still haven't told us how we find those Indians," she said.

"I told you. You got to learn to dream first."

Her eyebrows went up. "And you won't give us directions?"

"You got eyes. Use them," Trueblood said. "Suppose you come on a clearing where corn's been planted. Corn is their main food, or used to be. They had twenty, thirty different ways to use it: corn bread, corn pudding, smoked and dried and cracked and ground. And when they finished with the part you eat, they used the cobs for scrubbing things and chunked off pieces to make stoppers. Husks they burned for fuel or they make dolls for their children."

"You mean there are *cornfields* out there in the woods?" Lexi didn't believe it. "How could there be without people stumbling onto them?"

Ignoring her question, Trueblood continued, "You want signs? Find a rock with a crack chiseled out to hold a nut for cracking. Find the stone they used to pound the corn, or scrapers they used to clean animal hides, maybe a scrap of basket or a stone mask. Look for what don't fit in the woods. Then if you learn to dream right, those Indians'll maybe let you find them.'

"And then what will they do with us?" she asked.

"Oh, they'll feed you. They treat guests well. Besides, you're kids. *Maybe* they'll adopt you if you're good enough. You got to trust, girl," Trueblood said. "You want to belong to anything, you got to learn to trust."

"Thanks, Trueblood," Jeb burst out. "I guess we got everything so we can leave anytime." He looked eager enough to start out right then.

"What about food?" Trueblood asked him. "Might be days before you find them."

"Well, I stashed a jar of peanut butter and some crackers in the barn," Jeb said.

Trueblood chuckled. "I got some trail mix. Costs though. You got more where that five dollars is, girl?"

"We need more than peanut butter, Jeb," Lexi said to her cousin. "How about soup mix that we could add to water, and dried fruit and cereal maybe?"

"What we need most is a compass," Jeb said, "in case we get lost."

"How about a map?" Trueblood mocked him. "How about a map with an *x* marking the spot where the Indians are hiding?"

She narrowed her eyes at him and accused, "I bet you're sending us on a wild goose chase. I'll bet there isn't anything in those woods except a few raccoon and some deer."

"You're right," Trueblood said. *"You're* not going to find anything, nothing that you haven't dreamed."

Jeb gripped her hand on the way back to the farm. "Lexi," he said, "I found a stone mask once, a part of a one. It was from the False Face Society when they made somebody well by chasing the evil spirit out of him."

"Where is it?"

"Jim borrowed it to show his teacher and I never got it back."

"Did you ask the teacher?"

He shrugged. "Anyway, tomorrow the shellac'll be dry on the wood and we'll go . . . if you're still coming with me."

"I am," she said. "But when we go back to buy the supplies, let's try again to get Trueblood to draw us a map or something. You're his friend. He should do that for you."

"I don't know. I don't think he wants to," Jeb said.

She didn't think so, either. But even if the stone mask wasn't real, and even if she didn't dream the right dream, she wanted to go with Jeb. No matter what they found, it would be an adventure.

"Lexi, you got home just in time," Aunt Jane said when Lexi walked into the kitchen. "My friend Ethel just landed in the hospital and I got to see to her baby. You want to watch this soup I'm cooking and throw in some noodles and sausage in an hour? And that'll take care of supper. Okay?"

"Sure," Lexi said. She had expected to be late for dinner and here she was the first one home and in charge of it instead, but she welcomed another chance to prove that she was capable.

"Tell the girls I'm at Ethel's and I'll eat there. They went to some meeting about the church centennial. Should be home soon." She grabbed her overstuffed black leather purse and was out the back door.

A minute later Lexi heard the car engine. She surveyed the sink, which was full of potato and carrot peelings, and began cleaning it out.

"What are you up to?" Jesse asked. She and Janet came in dressed in identical blue skirts with different-colored shirts.

"Your mother had to help out a friend, so I'm finishing supper."

"You?" Jesse said. "She left *you* to make our supper?"

Lexi didn't answer. She turned back to the sink, gritting her teeth to hold back her temper.

Janet lowered the heat under the pot just as it began to boil over. "Where'd Ma go?" she asked.

"Her friend Ethel's," Lexi said. "Something about having to take care of her baby."

"Oh, Ethel. She needs rescuing at least once a week," Janet said.

"Why don't you go read or something, Lexi," Jesse said after tasting the soup. "We'll finish this up." She shook in some salt and opened the spice cabinet.

"Why are you both wearing the same skirt?" Lexi asked, annoyed enough to risk a dig at them.

"It was a 4-H project," Janet said without taking offense. "We picked the same pattern so we wouldn't have to buy more than one, and Ma had the cloth."

"You look like twins," Lexi said.

She had meant it as a taunt, but Janet only smiled. "Yeah," she said. "We know."

"Janet and me always wanted to be twins," Jesse said.

Lexi gave up in disgust and left the kitchen to them. No Indian could be less familiar to her than these girl cousins. She didn't feel like reading. She was standing in the middle of the living room trying to decide what she did want to do when Jim and Joe tore through it.

"Gimme that, gimme that, Jim. It's mine," Joe was yelling.

"She says she likes you a lot. She says she loooooves you," Jim said from the stairs. He pressed the slip of paper he was holding to his heart.

"That's my note. You show that to anyone and I'll kill you," Joe screeched. He tore up the stairs after his brother, who was cackling in glee. The upstairs door slammed. Immediately Joe began pounding on it.

Uncle Jake opened the front door. He walked unsteadily to the largest armchair and sat down. Then he focused or tried to focus his eyes on Lexi. "Am I in the wrong house?" he asked.

"I don't think so, Uncle Jake."

"Well, who are you?"

She moved close to him in concern that something was wrong with him. Then she smelled the liquor on his breath. Suddenly it was all too much. This was the family she had chosen to come to, to belong to, her flesh and blood. Her eyes filled up with tears. "I'm your niece," she said, and fled upstairs to her bed. She picked up Tolkien and held it against her chest. "Take it easy," she told herself. "Pretend you're an Indian. Indians don't cry. At least so Trueblood would claim."

Trust. Trust and dream. Maybe he was right. Was it her own fault that she didn't belong, that the dearest friend she'd ever had was a gentle black man who was now dead? She muffled her tears in the pillow. Much later she woke up in the dark. She was hungry, and she couldn't remember her dream.

7

Trueblood was glad enough to sell them the ten dollars worth of supplies Lexi chose, but he balked when
she asked if he'd draw them a map.

"But where did you see the signs, Trueblood?" Jeb
asked. "You can tell us that, can't you?"

"Even if I told you, you'd never find nothing."

"Then why are you selling us all this stuff if we haven't
got a chance?" Lexi asked. "Do you want us to get lost?"

"You're the ones want to try it, not me," Trueblood
said.

Lexi sighed. "How far should we go on the river?" she
asked.

"You got to stop before the rapids," he told her grudgingly. "There's a stream comes in there that you got to follow."

"How far?" Lexi asked.

Trueblood shook his head. "I'm telling you you can't find them."

"Why not?" Jeb asked.

"Because you're just kids. I had to climb a cliff. Yeah. Took me hours and I nearly fell off. That would have been the end of me. Nobody'd ever find my bones there in the woods, supposing anybody'd bother looking."

"A cliff?" Lexi asked. "Did you see them from the top of the cliff?"

"I saw something."

"What?" Jeb demanded.

"Lots of treetops . . . and behind the rock was a cleared space down in the woods where corn was growing."

"And Indians were down there?" Jeb asked.

"Who do you think's going to grow corn in the middle of nowhere without a town or electricity or anything in ten miles?" Trueblood snapped.

"What about a hermit?" Lexi suggested.

"A hermit?" Trueblood sounded angry. "This was Indian corn. You think I can't tell the difference between a field some crazed white man plants and corn an Indian grows for his life's blood?" He turned his back on them. "Go on home now," he growled.

"Please, Trueblood," Jeb begged. "What'd the cliff look like?"

"No. That's enough. You want to join them Indians, find them yourself."

But Jeb wouldn't give up. He said, "I only heard about one place near here that's high up, and that's Bird Cliff. Is it Bird Cliff, Trueblood?"

"Bird Cliff. Yes, and you can't climb it. Even if you could get to it, you can't. It goes straight up to the beak part, and the toeholds are too far apart for a kid."

"You said the cornfield was below the cliff," Jeb said.

"Right. Back there behind the mountain where nobody's going to see it except they climb that cliff. And nobody's fool enough to try that—except me."

"Do you think it's a big tribe?" Lexi asked.

"More like a family, a handful of people. But you never know." Trueblood's eyes were farseeing and dreamy. "Maybe there's a big tribe. Maybe. They're Turtle Clan though, that I know."

"How do you know?" Lexi asked.

He looked at her with his strange lopsided smile. "Where do you think I found the clan sign I got hanging by my door?"

"You made it. We saw you."

"Not that one. That one I found."

Lexi and Jeb both stepped outside to examine the roughly carved wooden turtle again. It seemed to Lexi that yesterday he had clearly said he was going to hang the carving he was making beside the door. But it did look different today, blackened by age or something. She looked at Jeb. He was staring at the turtle reverently. Trueblood stood behind them.

"Where's the one you were carving?" Lexi asked.

"I sold it to a fella been bugging me to make him one."

On the way home, Jeb sparkled with energy. Lexi said doubtfully, "He says we can't climb that cliff, Jeb. Maybe we can't."

"Don't have to," Jeb said. "All's we got to do is climb around behind it and look for the cornfield."

"We didn't ask him *when* he saw it. It could have been years ago."

"He's only lived here a couple of years. . . . You don't have to come."

"I want to," she said.

"Well, then, let's get the raft and go."

"Now?"

"We're ready, aren't we?"

"Yes," she agreed. They were ready.

Jeb's excitement infected her as they hurried home, and she found herself grinning for no reason. In the barn they surveyed the raft, which looked substantial in the dim light. Her only comment was, "We have to leave them a note."

"What if they decide to come after us?" Jeb asked.

"Will they if we just say we're going camping for a few days?"

"Maybe not, but Ma won't like it," Jeb said. "One rule she makes us stick by is we sleep in our own beds."

"Really? What about sleep-overs? Don't Jesse and Janet go to their girlfriends' houses sometimes?"

"They don't have girlfriends, just each other."

"You mean, you've really never slept anywhere but in your own bed?" Lexi asked. He drew into himself, but she hadn't meant to mock him. "What if you get home-sick, Jeb?"

"I won't. Sleeping in my bed's not that great. My brothers are always slipping ice cubes under the covers or dropping a mess of worms on my face in the middle of the night."

She laughed. "Your brothers are awful."

"Not to each other." Jeb sounded so wistful that Lexi was reminded that she wasn't the only one with a need to belong. "You write the note then," he said.

"Worried about getting in trouble?"

He shrugged, looking embarrassed. "My writing's so bad nobody can read it," he said.

"But you're good in school, Jeb, aren't you?"

"I told you. I'm not good at anything," he said.

She wondered how he dared set forth on this adventure with so little faith in himself. "I think you are," she said. "Would I go with you if I didn't think you were smart and strong?"

"I guess," he said with a shy smile. But he repeated, "You write the note, Lexi," and she agreed.

They would try out his raft, and assuming it didn't sink immediately, they would explore the river on it. She was eager to experience the river and woods and hills, to see and touch and smell and hear them, to absorb this place into herself so that it became hers to draw on whenever she wished. Whether they found Indians or not, eventually she expected to return. She was not too concerned about her aunt and uncle's anger. What could they do to her? Ship her back to her parents? She'd be glad enough of that. She missed her parents, the smell of Dad's pipe and his rumbling voice explaining things to her, even the familiar sight of her mother's prim profile bent over her needlework.

To write the note, Lexi had to go back to the house for paper and pen. "Anything else I should get for the trip?" she asked Jeb.

"Not that I can think of." He had a Boy Scout knife, and matches in a waterproof box in his pockets. Their food, including what she'd bought from Trueblood, was in a plastic bag along with a clothesline to tie up the raft or repair it. "What else do you think we need?" he asked.

"Sleeping bags and toothbrushes and soap," she said immediately.

He shook his head. "Jim's got a sleeping bag, but I'm not taking it."

"What about blankets then?"

"No, Lexi. They'll get wet, and besides, we put too much weight on this raft and we'll be under water before we start."

"It gets cold in the woods at night, doesn't it?"

He frowned. "Yeah. But Indians don't have sleeping bags."

"So how do they keep warm?" Last night she had awakened, shivering, to find her blanket had fallen off, and that was inside a house.

"Indians can take the cold."

"But we're not Indians yet. Think of something."

"I don't know."

"And what if it rains?"

"We'll get wet."

"Umm." She imagined being cold and wet. Well, if Jeb could take it, so could she. Hadn't her father said she was tough? And what was an adventure unless something had to be overcome? "I'll see what I can find in the house. You check out the barn for anything we can use."

"What are you going to tell Janet and Jesse?"

"Nothing. Don't worry. We'll leave the note here in the barn."

Her cousins were—where else—in the kitchen. She could hear their voices, Janet saying, "Your bride looks like she's scared."

"Well, if you don't like the way I draw, you do it, Janet."

"No, that's okay. A bride could be scared. . . ."

Smiling to herself, Lexi tiptoed up the stairs. The first thing she went for was her toothbrush and toothpaste. Then she checked out the medicine cabinet and found some antiseptic cream and Band-Aids. She thought of toilet paper but decided Jeb would not approve. No Indian used toilet paper. What then? Leaves? Just in case, she wadded up a handful of facial tissues and stuck them in her jeans pocket. She took a heavy sweater from her suitcase, wrote the note, and put that in her pocket.

On the shelves in the hall where Jesse's dolls were displayed were boxes of miscellaneous things. She needed something light and warm and waterproof. Her eye lit on an open box of plastic lawn and leaf bags. If it rained, they might come in handy. She took out six bags and ran on tiptoe down the stairs and out of the house.

Grass and trees shone green-gold in the sunlight. Lexi's spirits shone with them. They were off. They were off and she didn't have to spend another minute sitting indoors making herself do what she didn't do well.

In the barn, she called, "Jeb, I'm ready," and stuck the note onto a nail protruding from a beam.

Jeb tied the rest of the supplies she'd brought onto the raft. "They better not be looking out the windows," he said as Lexi helped him shove open both barn doors and pull the raft outside.

"It's heavy," she said. "If it sinks, can we go by foot?"

"To Bird Cliff? It's too far, I think." He glanced uneasily at the house, but she wasn't worried. Jesse and Janet were too absorbed in their project to look up. Jeb's brothers had left for the ball field after breakfast and couldn't be expected to return until they got hungry sometime this afternoon. His parents were both at work.

While they were dragging the raft toward the river, she said, "If the girls at Thistlewood could see me now, they'd say, 'there she goes again, acting like a boy.' I feel female, but I guess I do better with males."

"I don't do well with anybody," Jeb said.

"Even in your family?"

He frowned. "Well, Mom likes me sometimes."

"And who do you like?"

"You, if you were my sister," he said. She was startled and so pleased she almost missed his explanation. "Janet's okay, and Jesse's nice sometimes. Joe's not bad when Jim's not around. Jim's the one that gives me the hardest time. He's just never liked me much. He liked Joe even when he was a baby before he could play ball."

Jeb sounded so sad. To comfort him, she said, "Maybe Jim'll like you when you're both older."

"I doubt it."

"I always wanted a brother or sister," she confided.

"Want to tell the Indians we're brother and sister?" he asked.

"We have to learn their language before we can tell them anything," she said.

"You don't think they'll know English?" He thought about it. "Yeah, maybe not. We'll have to talk in sign language."

"Ug," she said playfully. "Me Lexi. Him brother Jeb."

Jeb grinned. "You could braid your hair. You'd look sort of like a squaw then."

They stopped to rest several times. The raft was so heavy Lexi suggested that they leave the supplies and return for them after they'd hauled the raft to the river, but he insisted they push on. "We're nearly there," he said. Once they had to unload to seesaw their burden over a wire strung fence. Finally, they made it. She looked down at the river from a high, undercut bank.

"I don't think the shellac's dry yet, Jeb." She showed him her fingers, sticky from grasping the wood.

"Well, we can't go back now," he said.

A branch sailed by with a leaf fluttering from it like a miniature sail. "That current looks really strong," she said.

"Yeah, it should carry us downstream fast. See we had so much rain this spring that the river's swollen. Midsummer the level will drop and the water'll slow down."

"We can't get on it from here, can we?" she asked.

"No. There's a low spot down a ways where my dad has a rowboat. It'd be easier to launch her there. Can you haul this thing a few more yards?"

"Sure," she said, gamely. The ache in her arms and shoulders could be ignored a while longer.

They bumped the raft over a field of small rocks, prickly plants, and flowers. Daisies were the only ones Lexi recognized. "Why don't we borrow Uncle Jake's rowboat?" she asked.

"Can't. It's rotted out."

The spot where the decayed rowboat lay was a lot further than Jeb had promised. The joints of Lexi's arms were burning by the time they'd detoured past the last clump of bushes and edged their clumsy craft out to the river again.

"Okay," he said. "Let's try it."

He took off his sneakers, rolled up his jeans and walked into the water, pulling the raft after him, or trying to. "Can you lift your side some?" he asked. She unloaded the raft and exerted her strained muscles one more time, managing to heave the raft toward him. To her relief the six by ten-foot framework did float.

"Can you load the stuff back on while I hold it here?" he asked.

Dutifully, she brought the heaviest bag to him, the one with the food in it, then the bag with her things. The last bag felt oddly bony. The bow, it was the bow and arrows. "Are these Trueblood's? Did he give them to you?" she asked in surprise.

"Not exactly," Jeb said, and without explaining further, he climbed aboard his raft. It tipped under the water but steadied and rose up again as he moved toward the middle. "Get on, Lexi."

"I will not," she said. "You're a thief. I'm not going anywhere with you." She thought of the first time she'd doubted his honesty about Jim's lumber.

"No. No, really. It's okay," Jeb said. "See, Indians share everything, and Trueblood's an Indian, and you and me, we will be, too. That's why the early settlers thought Indians were thieves, because they'd just take what they needed without asking. But they weren't stealing. It's just their way."

"Trueblood may be an Indian, but he's not big on sharing," Lexi said. "He's not going to like it that you took his bow and arrow."

"When we don't need it, I'll send it back to him somehow."

More likely bring it back in a day or two, she thought. She climbed aboard, getting her sneakers and the bottoms of her jeans wet. Well, they'd dry. There was a lively breeze, and it felt as if it would be a warm day, at least in the middle of the river.

He shoved them off from the bank with a paddle. They began to move, slowly at first, then more quickly as they swung into the current. It struck her that the current only went one way. "Jeb, if we don't find those Indians, how will we get back?"

"By paddling," he said.

Somehow she doubted it. Walking would be more likely. She took off the sweater which she'd tied around her waist.

"Isn't this great?" he asked. "Isn't it?"

"Awesome," she said. "You built a good raft, Jeb."

He grinned at her proudly and handed her one paddle. He was standing up, steering with the other. The raft zigzagged as he dug into the water. "You better use the paddle on your side," he said.

The only time she'd ever used a paddle or oar was on a rowboat on Central Park Lake in New York City when her father had let her help him row. But she dug into the water confidently, bent her knees, shoved and nearly fell on her nose. The water felt thick and resistant.

"Just stick the blade in, not the whole thing," Jeb said. "Look." He showed her. Meanwhile they had swung completely around and were hung up under a bush against the bank.

Lexi clawed her way out of the branches that were caging her and knelt to try to use just the blade. Nothing happened. Jeb moved cautiously toward her side. The unbalanced weight made the raft tilt up out of the water. "Move to where I was," he said. She moved and the raft leveled.

He pushed his oar against the bank, using a convenient rock as a lever to get them turned back into the main current again. A crow flew overhead cawing at them either in warning or complaint. The river had seemed tamer from shore, Lexi thought. Now they were in a tunnel of solid green with a narrow opening to the sky overhead. They could drown with no one around to save them. She shushed her fear. Adventure meant risking. She wasn't being shot at, was she? She could swim, couldn't she?

"We did it, Lexi. We're on our way," Jeb crowed.

His exuberance made her smile. "Do you know where to stop?" she asked.

"Well, we go under the railroad bridge, and then a ways further and when we come to the rapids, we pull in to shore."

"You've seen these rapids?"

"Well, no, but I know about where they are . . . I think."

She laughed and cut loose her fears. They would face whatever challenges were to come when they had to.

Meanwhile they were, as Jeb said, on their way. A brown shack with a rusty car beside it passed them on the left bank of the river, and on the right, along came a white, shingled house with a porch stacked with firewood. A single lawn chair waited in a yard that sloped to a dock where a motorboat was tied. It seemed less than a minute before the house was out of sight behind them. The current was whipping them right along.

"Oh-oh," Jeb said. "I forgot the presents. We got nothing to give them when we meet them. How are they going to know we're their friends?"

"Well, we're kids. Kids aren't likely to be enemies," she reasoned.

"But I had beads and stuff, beads and mirrors and a magnifying glass. I been hiding it in the barn so long I forgot. We got to go back, Lexi. We need that stuff."

She shook her head. "Too late, Jeb. Forget it." But he faced the other way and began trying to paddle back. His efforts didn't even slow the raft.

"Row, Lexi," he said. He bent his thin back to the task. She forced her blade through the water, and the raft turned slightly, but continued with the current. She pushed the blade through the water as hard as she could. It was like trying to turn a moving car by pushing on the fender.

"We can't do it," she said.

He struggled another minute before he gave up.

"Okay," he said. "Let's just pull into shore and I'll walk back."

But the stream had narrowed and was flowing even faster. "Pull hard," he yelled. They both paddled toward shore with all their strength. The runaway raft slid sideways through the water, going with the superior force of the current. Trees rushed by on either bank, then bare ground where the only growth seemed to be gray boulders, smooth gray stone slabs that were cracked and etched with pale green lichen. In silence they accepted the fact that the river was in control.

"If we don't find any Indians, we'll just hike home," Lexi said.

"Yeah, if we don't get adopted, I guess. I hope Trueblood doesn't get too mad about the bow and arrows. I figured we needed something to hunt with, I mean for after the food we've got is gone."

"You're going to kill deer?" she asked him.

"Well, rabbits, maybe, or squirrels."

"Are you a good hunter?"

"Uh, well, I've never killed anything, but I can shoot pretty good. I've been practicing in the barn."

She knew that. "Look," Lexi pointed at a four-foot-high bird standing in the shallows. It took alarm at their passage and ran on bamboo legs, spreading out great grey wings. When it took flight, its legs and long neck folded under it like landing gear. Exotic as it was, it reminded her of Africa. "Heron?" she asked.

"Great blue," he said. "You see them on the river sometimes."

Her eyes followed the bird until the treetops hid it. Already this placid landscape was charming her.

"We're coming up to the railroad bridge," Jeb said. "You better get down. It's low."

They were under the bridge and past before Lexi realized how they could have used it. "We should have stuck up our paddles to stop ourselves."

"Maybe," he said. "Anyway, we're too far now to go back. Let's hope they take us in without the presents."

Jeb was so positive there were Indians. Now that they were actually on the river on a raft that he'd built, she was starting to believe it, too—not a whole tribe surely, but a few hermit Indians hiding in those hills, keeping their distance from white society. How would they look on a pair of their enemies' children? First things first, she told herself. The river had them now.

They hadn't passed any houses in a while. The woods looked wilder. The river was wider and shallower here and the mountains loomed closer. Looking down, Lexi could see plate-sized stones—how many feet down? Five, three—it was hard to tell and they were still moving fast.

"What's that?" she asked when she first heard the

sound, like a subway roar, like the clattering of many feet.

"I guess that's the rapids," he said. "We better find that side stream to turn into." He was peering anxiously at the riverbank, afraid they might not be able to turn the raft, afraid they might miss the stream. Seeing that he was scared somehow made her calm.

"Will it be to our left or right?"

"I don't know," he said. "I never—"

"Been this far," they finished together. Silently they positioned themselves, each on his own side of the raft with the paddle at the ready. The rapids were shouting now, shouting like the crow had, but this time Lexi had no doubt it was in warning.

Suddenly the muscular brown water was throwing up white crests of foam. Whole tree trunks seemed to be snagged on rocks around them, and ahead the rolling water looked angrier yet.

"Use your paddle. Push off the rocks," Jeb said. His eyes showed white with fear. He grabbed for the plastic bag with Trueblood's bow and arrow. Lexi tied her bag around the end of her paddle. Her nerves coiled for action and her heart drummed in her ears. She glimpsed a small stream to her left just as the raft jolted against a hidden obstacle and tipped up.

Cold water enveloped her. Clinging to her paddle, she

kicked her way up to the air and found herself in a quiet backwater on the far side of the submerged rock that had upset their raft. A piece of the broken raft careened off to midstream. Her eyes followed it, and she saw an arm lift above the surface. Jeb! He couldn't swim. He was twenty feet away and drowning. She threw her paddle onto shore and scrambled after it through soft mud. She yanked off plastic bag and ran along the bank with the paddle in hand.

As soon as she was as close to Jeb as she could get by land, she called to him, reaching out with the paddle, but he was still too far away to grasp it. He went under again. When he surfaced, his face was blank and unseeing. She threw the paddle ahead of her into the stream and did a shallow dive after it. The chilly water was deep here, but at least they were out of the current. She swam to the paddle and pulled it along to Jeb. When she reached him, she lifted him up by his hair, fitting the pole under his chin.

"Hang on to it," she told him, but though his eyes were open, he didn't seem to understand her. She was treading water, clutching the paddle and his hair. "Jeb, help me," she begged.

His hand came up and took hold. His other hand came up clamped on to the bag with Trueblood's bow and arrows. She turned and did a one-armed sidestroke to shore, pulling the paddle along and scissor kicking. When she hauled him out, Jeb lay face down in the mud. She thought he had drowned.

"Jeb," she shook him. "Come on, wake up."

He was heavier than she was, but she rolled him over a nearby log. Then she pushed with the heels of her hands against the small of his back. Water gushed from his mouth. She released the pressure and pumped again and again until the water stopped coming. Finally she lifted and tugged at him until she had him propped against the log in a sitting position. "Jeb, are you alive?"

She saw his chest move. Relief filled her. He was breathing. She lay back and let the sun warm her wet, chilled body. Exhausted, she rested for a long time.

When she felt better, she opened her eyes and found him sitting there beside her. "You saved my life," he said solemnly.

She sighed. "You better learn to swim, Jeb."

"You saved my life," he repeated.

"Well, I sure wasn't going looking for these Indians by myself." She smiled at him.

"I don't know," he said. "We lost the food bag. Maybe we better just go home. We could try again in July when the river slows down."

"Good idea," she agreed. "I could use a hot bath and some lunch." She stood up. She felt okay, hungry, but okay. They had had enough of an adventure for one day.

"So what do you think?" she asked. "We can't get lost if we follow the river back upstream. Only we'll be on the wrong side when we get there."

"We can cross by the railroad bridge."

"Oh, right. Then let's start."

They started. But it wasn't that simple. They were not only on the wrong side of the river, they were on the far side of the stream that fed the river, the one Jeb had planned for them to swing into. They followed it, detouring around clumps of brush that got in the way, searching for a spot that looked shallow enough so that they could wade across it.

"Look," Lexi said, after they'd walked a long while. "We're just knocking ourselves out and wasting time going in the wrong direction. Why don't I see if we can ford this stream. It isn't as scary as the river. The water's barely moving."

"It looks deep," he said anxiously, "and I'm not getting in water over my head again. No way." He shivered.

She would have taunted him about losing his Indian courage, but she saw how overwhelming his fear was. He had almost drowned. "You could hold on to the paddle and I could tow you across," she said.

"No." He shook his head so stubbornly that she gave up the idea. She wasn't eager to wade into the mud-dark stream, anyway. She hated touching bottoms she couldn't see, especially squishy bottoms where snakes might be hiding or unknown slimy creatures.

They kept walking. "Look." In delight, Lexi pointed at a beaver waddling down to the water with a stick in its jaws. It slipped into the stream and with a flap of its broad tail went under.

"Lots of beaver around here," Jeb said.

"I wish we had time to look for his lodge," she said. "It would be fun to watch him build, wouldn't it?"

"Well, but it'd be mostly underwater," Jeb said.

Movement in a pocket of water behind a cluster of rocks by the stream's edge caught her eye. "There's fish in there," she said. She sat down, chin on her hand. "You didn't bring a hook and string, did you?"

"Nah. I should have thought of it. But I didn't." He sat down beside her.

"What about the matches? You still have them?"

He reached into his pocket and brought out first the folding knife and then a plastic soap dish with the matches. They seemed dry. "Jeb," she said, "why don't you get a fire started, while I think of how to catch this fish. We're not likely to make it back before dark, and we need to eat something to keep up our strength."

"I'm sorry I lost the food bag," he apologized. "All that money you paid for that stuff." He shook his head.

"Not your fault."

"Yeah, it was. I should have built the raft stronger so

it wouldn't break up. Well, I'll make a fire." He went off and presently came back with an armload of small dead branches.

The only things she had to trap the fish in were plastic bags. What if she could lure it into the center of the shallow pocket of water, then shunt it into a bag which she could stretch across the outlet between the pocket and the stream. She weighted the bottom of a plastic bag with rocks, wedged a stick across the top to hold it open, then laid the stick on the water with the edge of the bag rolled back to keep it in place. It made a sloppy, partial opening. She moved off a few feet and found a dish-sized stone. Under it were some grubs. Gingerly she scooped them up, mud and all, carried them to the pool and dropped them in, hoping the fish would come out to investigate. The mud discolored the water so that she couldn't see anything in it. No movement now. She stuck her hand in and touched something live. Acting on reflex she grabbed and pulled out a grey fish the size of her forearm.

"Jeb," she yelled. She threw the stunned fish away from the bank so that it couldn't flop back into the water. Jeb gave a whoop and smacked it with a branch. It lay still.

"You caught a sucker!" Jeb looked at Lexi in awe. "How'd you do it?"

"Just luck," she said. "After I grabbed it, I thought it might be a snake and I panicked. Good thing you were here. Can we eat it?"

"Sure, you can eat suckers." He returned to his fire building.

She retrieved the plastic bag from the river. It hadn't done its part, but she still had faith in the benefits of modern technology. The plastic bags had to be useful for something. They were all she had to survive with besides her toothbrush and toothpaste, Band-Aids and antiseptic cream, and the wad of wet facial tissues. She'd lost her sweater somehow when the raft cracked apart. Luckily, she'd put her sneakers back on or she'd have lost them, too. She swatted the mosquitoes that had found her out and looked at the sucker, hoping it had enough meat in it for two people.

"How's the fire coming?" she asked Jeb.

"Just smoking," he mumbled. "I think the wood's wet or something." A while later, he'd used up half his match supply and the fire was still smoking. Jeb looked at her guiltily. He wasn't managing his part of this meal and he knew it.

She began picking apart the wet facial tissues and spreading each one out to dry on a sun-heated rock. The rock cooked them rapidly. "Here," she said. "Maybe these will burn."

He took the three tissues and tucked them under the small twigs he'd been using as tinder. Sure enough the tissues flamed up in an instant, and this time the twigs caught fire. He cooked the fish whole on a stick over the fire, then got out his knife and split and deboned the sucker. They ate it with their fingers. By the time they'd finished, the sun was angled at the trees on the opposite bank and they were in shade.

"Boy, that tasted good," Jeb said.

"Not bad," Lexi agreed. "Next time we'll bring salt."

He smiled. "Yeah, next time I'll remember." He pointed to the shadows cast by the trees. "Looks like we're heading west if we follow this stream. It could be dark before we can turn the right way. We better get going."

"What's the hurry? We can camp like we planned and get home tomorrow morning," she said.

"Well, but we're heading west and home's more like southeast from here. We're just getting farther and farther away, Lexi."

"Then let's ford this stream and go in the right direction."

He shook his head stubbornly and began walking, searching again for a likely spot to cross. Lexi ventured into the water a couple of times, with her pants legs rolled up, but the bottom was mucky and the water deepened fast. She was about to say that, like it or not, he would have to let her try to swim across, towing him behind, when he abruptly stopped short.

"Lexi, I found it."

"What?"

"A sign." His voice rang with excitement. He picked up a stone fixed to a wooden handle by dark colored lacing that had mostly rotted away. "An Indian made this. It's just like one Trueblood showed me."

She studied the oblong stone. A crease appeared to have been gouged around it so that the lacing would hold in place. Not something the local hardware store would carry. But the lacing was string. "Shouldn't this be leather?" she asked, pointing to what remained.

"Well, maybe they found some string. They're going to use what they find, even if it isn't something from the old days, right? It'd be dumb not to, and these guys can't be dumb and survive here."

"I guess. So now what?"

He looked up at the steep slope beside them to a rock outcropping that interrupted the green needle and leaf screen between them and the mountain's face. "That could be Bird Cliff. It's hard to tell from down here."

"Really?" It would be foolish not to continue if just over the hill were an encampment of Indians willing to take them in. Her tiredness left her. Jeb put the stone tool in the bag with the bow and arrows. "Lead on," she told him. He did with such energy that she fell behind and had to scramble after him. "Don't you ever wear out?" she asked.

"Sorry," he said, and thereafter led the way more slowly.

She had finally beaten through the denser growth along the stream bank. Now she was scrabbling on hands and knees up the smooth face of the cracked and lichen-covered gray mass that had looked like a rock from below but seemed to stretch on forever as they climbed. He was standing on top. He gave her a hand up. She lay flat on the rock, too exhausted to sit up.

"I'm sorry," he said. "This isn't Bird Cliff. You want to rest awhile?"

"Let's just camp here," she said. "I can't move another step." He sat patiently beside her. In a few minutes she felt better and sat up. "Well, the view's nice," she said cheerfully when she'd looked around. They could see across the stream to the woods on the other side. The clouds made a white sculpture garden of giant mythical shapes above the trees. The only problem was that the tree tops seemed endless. No signs of civilization, no chimneys or roofs in either woods or sky, not even a jet passing by. "Are we lost, Jeb?" she asked.

"Not so long as we can follow the river, but it could take time to get home from here." Again he was sounding apologetic.

"Listen," she said, "it's not your fault we're here. I wanted to come, and so far, we've had a great time."

"Well, but it's scary in the woods at night, and it'll be cold and we don't have any sleeping bags."

"Umm. There'll be a moon, won't there?" She lay back down, realizing that every joint in her body ached.

"Be right back," he said. "I'm going to scout around."

"Just don't get out of sight," she said.

"I won't. Yell if you can't see me. Okay?"

"Okay," she agreed, although she was uneasy about being left behind. He began climbing. As he approached the top of the mountain, the underbrush thinned out and it was easier to keep him in sight. Once he stopped. "Find anything?" she called.

He put his finger to his lips and waved her to come on. She rose with a groan, picked up both her bag and Jeb's, and made her way up the mountain toward him. "What?" she whispered.

He was looking at some plants. "Strawberries, and there's dandelions you can eat too," he said softly. "And look."

"At what? That feather? That doesn't mean anything, Jeb. Some bird could have dropped it."

"Maybe."

He didn't think so, she saw. It looked long enough to be an eagle feather. It might have been an Indian who lost it from his hair while he bent over to pick the berries. Or it could have been a bird. Didn't birds eat berries, too? "Anyway, this'll finish off our dinner. Let's eat," she said.

She was hungry, but it seemed to her that he had let her eat more than her fair share of the tart little berries. "Jeb, what're you thinking about?" she asked.

"If we see any little animals, this is the best time to shoot one," he said, "just before dark."

It was the best time for gnats, too. Lexi had to keep swatting at her head and face, and still the maddening insects gnawed at her. They even got into her hair and bit her scalp.

"I forgot the bug spray," he said woefully. He was swatting at the almost invisible cloud of pinhead-sized insects, too.

"I'm lost," she said. "Do you know where we are?"

"Well—sort of. I guess we should have left markers or something, but. . . . Let's camp when we get to the top. Then when it's light tomorrow, we can climb back down to the stream. We'll be okay I think."

He didn't sound too sure, but she followed him, trusting that it would work out. Behind them the sky was still bright with late afternoon, but they were climbing into heavy shadow. The only camping she'd ever done had been with her parents, snug in a sleeping bag in a tent with a flashlight beside her. She waved away the attacking squadrons of gnats in a hopeless gesture and clamped her lips shut. She would not be afraid. She would not.

In the dark, a long while later, she was tired of listening to the trip-hammer of her heart and the crunch of leaves and twigs underfoot. "Jeb, I have to rest again," she said.

He squatted where he was as if he were glad to rest, too. "I think this must be the top," he said.

"But we can't see anything."

"No, too many trees. We might as well camp here though."

"Fine." She surveyed the surrounding trees and rocks and low-growing juniper bushes and slapped a mosquito that was feasting on her neck. "What about animals?" she asked. "I mean, at night, is anything going to hunt us?"

"Well, there's bears, but you don't see them very often, and snakes don't come out at night. Owls hunt mice. We're too big."

"Indians," she said. "They hunt at night, don't they?"

"Want me to watch while you sleep?" he asked.

"No, thanks. You're tired too. We'll be okay, Jeb."

"Yeah, we'll be okay. But it's going to be really cold."

Without the sun it was cold all right, cold enough for her limbs to stiffen. She wished she hadn't lost that sweater. He didn't seem to feel it. At least he wasn't shivering the way she was. "Can you make another fire?" she asked.

"I'll try. But it's dangerous in the woods. We could

start a forest fire. I'll look for stones to put around it. Maybe you could help by clearing a space of stuff that could burn?"

"Sure," she said, adding, "don't go too far looking for stones."

"I won't. Can you whistle? I'll keep whistling, and if you whistle back—"

"Good idea." His whistle came comfortingly at regular intervals. She used bark slabs to scrape aside the litter of leaves, needles, and twigs. Tired as she was, she didn't mind the work. It called for different muscles than the ones she'd exhausted on the climb. He whistled. She whistled back. The wind was coming up now. Suddenly his whistle sounded far off. "Come back, Jeb," she yelled.

She could barely hear his answer. "This way," she yelled and was relieved when he emerged from the trees a minute later with his shirt stretched into a carrier for the stones. "I got scared," she admitted.

"It's scary in the woods at night," he said. He nodded at the cleared space she'd made. "You did a good job."

Looking at the piles of debris she'd scraped aside, she shivered. How cold did you have to get to die of exposure? But it was June. You didn't die of exposure in June, did you? But it was the mountains. And it was cold.

9

She wished they were camping in sight of the river. The river was a thread to lead them home through the labyrinth when morning came and they could see again. When morning came, they would find their way back to the thick brush that grew along the moist stream edge. The wind would bring them the sound of running water. The sun would come up in the east and they would walk toward it and eventually get back home.

He was stacking his firewood in the shape of a tepee. She brought him dead leaves and more twigs. Neither of them said much. He looked as cold and tired as she felt. He began dragging half a dead tree trunk to their fireplace, but when she went to help him, he said, "That's okay. I can do it."

"You're really strong, Jeb," she said. Her compliment seemed to renew his energy, and he got the trunk to the fire area.

"We'll put this on after we get the fire going good," he said. "It'll burn most of the night if we can get it going. You got any more of those tissues?"

Silently she offered him the last ones she had. They were dry by now. He crouched to light the fire. One match. Another match. Another. The last tissue flamed and went out without making the twig Jeb was nurturing catch fire.

"It should've worked," Jeb muttered guiltily. "I don't know why it didn't work. Maybe the wind's too strong or something. I don't know."

Lexi sneezed.

"You take my shirt," Jeb said, beginning to pull it off.

"No, that's okay. I'm not that cold."

"Do we have anything else we could burn?" he asked.

"How about your knife?"

"Huh?"

"If you scrape a piece of dry wood, the shavings might burn."

"Oh, yeah. Gee, you're smart, Lexi." He dug his knife from his pocket and began shaving the thickest stick they had found. A curl of wood fell from the stick and another and another. She tightened her arms around her bundled legs, trying to think warm thoughts. When the pile of shavings looked right to him, they knelt side by side to make a wind break as he struck one of the remaining matches against a stone. The wood shaving flamed up, and now the twig took. They fed the fire with care until it began consuming their wood supply at too rapid a rate. Lexi searched and found another dead branch, and another. Finally the bark on the dead tree trunk began smoking. At last they saw it burning.

"Wish we had some more of that fish," he said. "Or that peanut butter I lost in the river, or the soup or raisins."

His list made her mouth water. "Forget it," she said. "I bet your Indians went to sleep hungry plenty of times."

"They didn't eat as much as we do. One meal a day did it for them."

"I guess it's what you get used to," she said.

"Yeah." He sucked in his stomach, and she knew he was willing himself to be tough as an Indian. He took a deep breath and swallowed, his eyes on the fire.

"Tomorrow, you can try shooting something with the bow and arrows," she said.

"Yeah. If we can find anything to shoot. I haven't even seen a chipmunk."

"We've probably scared everything away," she said.

The fire was comforting. Lexi curled up close to it to sleep, but Jeb warned her to move back in case of flying sparks. Away from the fire, she immediately got cold again. The litter she had scraped aside felt soft, softer than the ground anyway. She thought of the plastic bags. "I wonder if we filled a leaf bag with leaves and pine needles, if it would act like a blanket," she said.

"Hmmm?"

"At least it would keep out the wind. It has to be better than nothing. Let's try it."

She gave him one of her plastic bags to fill and she took a second. They had to move out from the fire area to get enough loose material to stuff their bags. At first, everything they put in settled toward the bottom. Then Lexi broke a low branch off a juniper and laid that inside the plastic to act as a framework to hold the leaves and pine needles in place. As she foraged, she kept her eye on the fire for fear of getting lost.

The night sounds were more distinctive than the whispering of the leaves had been by day, more mysterious too. The swish and sigh of wind seemed louder. Something screeched and there was a low fluttering. It was easy to imagine that things could see her that she couldn't see, easy to imagine frightening shapes in the dark. She thought of Ezekiel who loved the dark, who said the dark freed his soul to become part of the night. Thinking of Ezekiel calmed her. Still, she was glad to return to the warmth of the fire. She huddled near the flames, using the bag as a shield behind her. It did keep off the wind at least.

Jeb came back. He lay down on the ground and fitted his bag over him like a lumpy blanket. "I think it helps," he said presently.

"Do you think your family's out looking for us?" she asked hopefully.

"What for? We said we were going camping. They won't worry for a few days. Then if we're not back, maybe they'll get the sheriff to send a search party after us."

"A few days? We better find our way back to that river in the morning. . . . We could boil the river water and drink it."

"I guess. But we only got four more matches. What we need's a mountain stream. That'd be cleaner than the river. Except they say there's some kind of germ even in little brooks in the woods that makes you sick."

She swallowed dryly and said, "I think I'd rather be sick than thirsty." Her teeth began chattering. The fire seemed to warm only a small part of her while the hunger at her center hollowed out her whole body.

"You know when we're going to enjoy this, Jeb? When we're home talking about how it was." She wanted to fall asleep, but she couldn't seem to get there. His eyes were open, too. "Tell me a story," she said. "Tell me about the book you were reading."

"I know a story Trueblood told me about the lost boy."

"So tell it to me."

"It's about brothers," Jeb said. "See, there was this little Onondaga boy who always got teased by his brothers, and they took him out hunting one time. So there was this hollow log, and they told him a rabbit was hiding in it. And they said he should crawl into the log. So he said, 'Why me?' And they said, 'Because you're the only one who's small enough to get in. You'll scare the rabbit and then we can kill it when it runs out the other side.' Well, so the little brother went in, but there wasn't any rabbit, and his brothers laughed at him, and they plugged the log at both ends so he couldn't get out. Then they went away.

"Well, so the brothers went home and told their parents the little kid was lost. And everybody went out searching for him, but they didn't find him, because he was a brave kid. So he didn't cry.

"And he would have died in that log except an old woman came and she sat on the log and called for her grandchild.

" 'I'm here,' the little kid said, but the old woman wasn't strong enough to get him out. So she said she'd be back with her children and they'd get him out. Well, she did, but when the boy got out of the log, he saw that the grandmother wasn't a person, but an old porcupine, and her children weren't people. They were Bear, Deer, and Wolf. So one of them was supposed to take the boy home with him.

"Well, the porcupine wouldn't let the wolf take the boy because she said he would eat him. She wouldn't let the deer take him because winter was coming and the deer had no home and the boy would die. But she let the bear take the boy to her cave because the bear was a loving mother, and the boy lived with the bear and was happy.

"Well, one day a hunter came and killed the mother bear. The boy called out to the hunter not to shoot him, and the hunter didn't because the hunter was the boy's father. See, he recognized his son. So the boy was very sad that his father had shot the bear that had been good to him, but his father said not to worry, that the bear's spirit was alive still and would always watch over him."

Jeb stopped talking.

Lexi thanked him and said, "That was so good it made me stop shivering."

"Trueblood tells lots of good stories," Jeb said, and he added, "I don't know why nobody likes him but me."

"How did you and he get to be friends?"

"Well, see what happened was people kept talking against him, like that maybe he was hiding out from the

119

law and had money hid somewhere. So some kids were going to break into his place one night to find the money, and I warned him."

"And what did he do?"

"He just waited, and when they came to his trailer he aimed his gun at them. He didn't say anything. He just stood there with the gun and they ran. But people didn't like it that he aimed the gun. Nobody trusts him except me. The way I see it, he's okay. He's just different, and people don't like you to be different."

"That's true," she said, thinking of Thistlewood.

"All I know is Trueblood's good to me," Jeb said. "Lots of times when I go over there, he'll sit and talk to me. He doesn't only know about Indians. He talks about stuff like cities. Like he lived in Tucson and Philadelphia. He says Philadelphia's his favorite because a minister was good to him there. And he tells me about women, and—my family doesn't tell me much."

"I can talk to my father," Lexi said. "When he has the time."

"What's he talk to you about?" Jeb asked curiously.

She thought about it. "Mostly about his work and what I'm learning, and sometimes about my mother, how bad she had it when she was a kid and lost her parents. . . . And I had a friend once—like you have Trueblood—his name was Ezekiel, and he talked to me about things like whether animals have souls, and if some people are born better than others."

"What'd he say about that, about some people being better?" Jeb asked.

"He said all people have a purpose and a place on earth and some are good and some evil, but everybody matters."

"Yeah, I like that," Jeb said.

"Me, too."

"If I'd been born an Indian, I'd be somebody good."

"You're already good, Jeb."

"Oh, yeah, sure. I'm just a goof up. Like the raft. Everything I do breaks up on the rocks."

"Why do you always think it's your fault?" she asked. "Nothing's wrong with you. You're just different. And so am I."

He was quiet after that for a while. Wings flapped overhead and something squeaked. "Owl," he said. And then he said, "When we get home, they're going to make fun of us for getting lost."

"So what? We'll tell them what a great adventure we had."

She closed her eyes and tried to sleep, but her mind was racing and she was shivering too hard. Suddenly she asked, "Do you think it's because of his scars?"

Jeb started. He must have been dozing. "What?"

"That people made up rumors about Trueblood because he's got those scars? He does look sort of scary."

"I think it's because he's a stranger."

"But he's lived here a couple of years."

"Around here they say that unless you've got more family in the cemetery than in your house, you're a stranger."

She sighed. So much for her dream of fitting in. She was a stranger to her cousins, and probably even the blood tie wouldn't change that. Maybe she would always be a fragment that didn't fit into a whole anywhere. She thought of her mother, who was a whole unto herself so long as she had her husband and her needlework and her kitchen.

"You don't care about me," Lexi had accused her once, years ago. "All you care about is Daddy."

"I care about you," Mother had said, "but you'll grow up and leave me. Your father, he'll stay."

Jeb was asleep. She could see his pale face resting on his hands above the plastic bag blanket on the other side of the fire. She removed a stick poking into her side, then dug out a rock from the ground under her hip. Moving dislodged her plastic bag blanket, and now she could feel the chill wind on her back. She rolled over so that her back was to the fire. For a while she dozed off.

She was back in a time when she'd ridden on her father's shoulders. They were scouting a dry riverbed in

Arizona for a certain kind of clay. "Look for a darker spot, a little reddish," he'd told her.

"There, Daddy." She pointed urgently.

"My sharp-eyed little monkey," he'd praised her. "Good thing I brought you with me." Had she been four or five? She couldn't have been older if he had been carrying her.

"You need to make friends your own age," he'd said last summer, when she had tried to convince him that she'd stay close to the house and out of the way of the soldiers. She hadn't wanted to leave him to go off to school in the States. "You need to make friends," he'd said. . . . So he'd wanted her to fit in somewhere, too. She'd have to write and tell him what she was discovering as she lay awake here, a revelation that was just forming itself into words.

A slice of lemony moon had drifted into the only open space in the canopy overhead. A branch cracked. Fear chased out her good feeling and she squinched her eyes shut. Something big was walking around out there. She ducked her head under her plastic cover, practically burying her nose in her chest. The back of her neck crawled with the sense that something, someone had come into the clearing. Terror froze her. A bear? They had no food to attract it. But bears sometimes attacked campers, bad bears out west. Hadn't she read about two girls mauled while they were sleeping? Oh, let the fire keep it away, please. She held her breath. Finally, she peeked. The figure bending over Jeb's sleeping body was human.

"Hey," she almost called to him. But what if he were an Indian? What if he came back with tomahawk raised and brought it down on her head? She held her breath until the body straightened. A man. A man she knew. Surprise took her breath away. "Trueblood," she nearly cried out then, but his stealth made her hesitate. Next thing she knew he stepped into the woods away from the firelight and vanished. Had she dreamed him? She heard a branch crack. He was leaving them. Why? Again she squelched the cry that would call him back. He obviously hadn't wanted them to know he'd come. How strange. She didn't understand it.

She got up, fully awake. She'd risk getting lost if she went much beyond the range of the fire, but the moon was bright. If she kept it shining over her left shoulder, then turned and kept it over her right shoulder returning, the fire should guide her back. She would go a little way, just a little way and see what she could see.

She crept along, keeping the moon in place and snatching reassuring glances of the fire over her shoulder. Remember the feel of this rock, this tree, this prickly bush, she told herself as she passed each. So cautiously did she creep that her movements seemed dreamlike and she wondered if she were really awake. Branches creaked in the wind, squeaked and rubbed against one another. What if Trueblood were watching her and suddenly jumped out at her! Fear chilled her and made the hairs on her arms rise. She stood still to quiet her breathing and to listen. She couldn't see anything, but that meant she couldn't be seen except by the owls and bats and other night creatures. A branch cracked a long ways off. Stupid to keep trekking after him through the woods. She'd never catch up. But why had he come to find them and then left them?

The moon. She touched her right shoulder. Her heart actually hurt, it was pounding so fast. There. The prickly bush was in the right place, and next came the rock, and yes, she could see the red glow of the burning log. Quickly she walked back to her plastic sleeping bag and got under it again. In no time, she was asleep.

When she woke up it was daylight. Jeb was smothering the last coals with dirt. "Hungry?" he asked.

"I'll say."

"I saw a rabbit, but I didn't shoot it. I was afraid of losing Trueblood's arrows."

"Didn't you say Indians shared?"

"Yeah, but Trueblood doesn't. I shouldn't have just taken the bow and arrows. I know it makes him really mad when kids snitch things from the store."

She wondered if it could be the bow and arrows that Trueblood had come for last night. It didn't seem likely, but she couldn't think of anything that *was* likely. She considered telling Jeb what she'd seen. Later, she thought. This was no time to tell him his friend had come and gone away without helping them. "So which way do we go?" she asked cheerfully.

"I'm not sure," Jeb said.

"Well, you're the pathfinder. Lead on," she said.

She couldn't tell which of his eyes exactly was looking at her, but in both of them she saw courage taking hold. They would need it, she thought, as she began emptying the plastic bags in case they needed to use them another night.

10

It would have been easy to walk toward the rising sun if the endless canopy of trees hadn't hidden it. "We've got to find a clearing," Jeb said. But there wasn't one. They walked downhill and found themselves in a ravine with no stream and no way out but up.

"I think the sun's coming from that way," Lexi said. She pointed to where a few rays slanted through holes in the greenery.

"Yeah, but we can't get through those bushes without getting all scratched up," Jeb said. He looked so worried that she didn't point out that they were both already covered with scratches.

127

By noon they were standing up to their knees in meadow grass speckled with thistles and daisies and clover. Surrounding them were woolly green mountains that all looked alike to Lexi.

"I bet you could plant corn here," Jeb said. "Maybe we'll find the Indians before we find our way home."

She was too tired to care much about Indians anymore. "Frankly I'd rather find a refrigerator stocked with food," she said.

"I'm sorry, Lexi."

"It's not your fault we're lost." It was Trueblood she blamed. Why hadn't he helped them? Unless he thought it would teach them a lesson. He had tried to discourage Jeb from searching for the tribe. Still, Trueblood had come after them, hadn't he? And she couldn't believe it was just to chase down his missing bow and arrows. Some other mission then. Suppose the hidden Indians and he were in contact and he brought them things in the night—aspirin and chewing gum, things they couldn't hunt or gather or grow in the woods. It wasn't likely, but then nothing she could think of was.

They crossed the meadow and found a stream. "Okay," Jeb said, "now we got something to follow."

She wanted to soak her feet in the water and rest awhile. She suggested he make a fire and they boil some water to drink, but he didn't want to take the time. "Look, it can't be that much further until we get to a house or a road, and then we can call home and ask them to come get us," he said.

"Jeb, I'm going to drink some of this water."

"You better not." He frowned at her, and then he pleaded, "I wish you wouldn't."

She was so thirsty and the water looked clear. "If I see a fish, I'm drinking, Jeb." They watched for a fish, but all they saw were bugs on the surface that he called water skaters and grasses that flowed like hair with the current.

The rest refreshed her. She didn't drink. "Okay," she said finally. "I'm ready. Let's see where this goes."

Where it went was a swamp. They tried to circle the margin of it, but a snarl of branches from low-growing trees blocked their way. Jeb thought he saw a hummock to step on and sank in mud to his waist. Besides that the mosquitoes and deerflies were fierce. Between trying to find a footing and slapping at their faces and arms and backs, it was hard to pay attention to where they were going.

"Watch out for snakes," Jeb said.

It was all Lexi had to hear. She faltered on the tree trunk that she was using to cross a mud patch and fell into it. Jeb helped haul her out. She was mud-coated even up to her hair and face.

"We got to get out of here," Jeb cried. He looked around wildly. The ground looked treacherous in every direction.

"Don't panic," she said. "We'll find a way out." Together they studied the jungle of willowy bushes and weedy hummocks surrounding them.

"I see pines," Jeb pointed. "They need solid ground to grow."

"Good. Let's head that way."

Slogging through knee-deep mud, they had almost made it when Jeb said, "Fiddlehead ferns." He pointed to a hummock and started for it. While she scrambled onto dry ground, he made a pocket of the bottom of his shirt and brought back what looked like thick, coiled grass stems to her. "Fiddlebacks're good to eat," he said. "Cooked they are, anyway."

"You're not going to make a fire, are you?" She didn't have much enthusiasm for any delay now that it was warm and sunny out.

"I guess we could eat them raw." He tried one.

"How is it?" She couldn't tell by his face. He shrugged and continued chewing. She took one to try. It tasted like grass to her. They each ate a couple. Then Lexi went off behind a bush to relieve herself. When she came back he grinned at her.

"What's funny?"

"You. You're all mud."

"Well, you're not too beautiful yourself," she said.

He laughed. "One thing about the mud is it keeps the bugs off you."

She was thinking that the bugs seemed to find her tasty, mud or no mud, when he stopped and said, "Lexi, look. There it is."

"What?" She looked where he was pointing and saw another rock formation. This one was high up above them; it had a chunk jutting out which looked like a bird's beak.

"We can still do it," he said. "We can still get there. It'll only take us an hour or two to get up to Bird Cliff. The Indians are closer than home is from here."

Somehow she didn't think so. Now was the time to tell him. "Jeb," she said, "Trueblood came to the fire last night. He looked at you but then he went away."

"Huh? He did? What did he say?"

"Nothing. He thought I was asleep, too, I guess."

"Well, what did you do?"

"Nothing. At first, I didn't know it was him. I was scared, and then . . . I don't know. He startled me and then he was gone."

"Why didn't you call after him?"

She didn't like admitting that she didn't trust Trueblood, that he made her uneasy. "Well," she said, "I went after him, but he disappeared so fast, and I didn't understand what was going on. I still don't."

"You were dreaming," Jeb said.

"No, I wasn't. I was wide awake and the moon was bright."

"You must've been dreaming, Lexi. Why'd he just leave us? He's my friend."

Exactly the question she'd been working on all morning without success. She said, "Jeb, don't go chasing after the Indians now. Let's go home. We can come back and try again. Aren't you hungry?"

"We can't come back. We lost the raft."

"Well, if we can walk home, why can't we walk back? If we had better camping equipment, we could stay out longer."

"The tribe'll feed us when we get to them. Don't make me go back yet, Lexi. Please."

There weren't any Indians. She was certain now, although she couldn't have explained what had convinced her. Still, she let him have his way. Until he'd investigated that cliff, he'd never be satisfied.

They walked on easily through park-like woods with little underbrush. Jeb wasn't saying any more about Trueblood. Probably he believed she had been dreaming last night, Lexi imagined, until he suddenly said, "Trueblood wouldn't of just left us there. Maybe it was an Indian that looked like him. In the dark, if you saw an Indian—"

"It was Trueblood."

Jeb sucked in his lips. He wasn't convinced but he wasn't going to waste time arguing. They crossed a cracked rock from which water was seeping, making the ground below it wet and spongy. "A spring," he said.

"We're lucky." They drank on their hands and knees like animals. Lexi even washed off some of the mud from her hands and face.

"The mosquitoes are going to get you," Jeb warned.

"I don't care." During the day few mosquitoes were around, anyway. Jeb was a blotchy mess of red bites. Judging by her arms, she was, too. "Your Indians are going to think we have measles or something," she said.

"See it?" he asked.

Under the pointing arm of a crooked evergreen, she saw a mass of boulders. Above that was the cliff. It rose in great, uneven slabs up and out to a jutting chunk of rock that looked as if it might crash into the valley at any minute. "You wait here," he said. "I'll climb as high as I can get on the back side and scout which way the field is."

"No," she said. "I'm coming with you."

"You're tired."

"So are you."

"I've been thinking," he said. "What if they don't want us?"

"Then we'll go home."

"But Lexi, if they don't want us, and they don't want anyone to find them, they might not let us go."

"Oh great," she said. "So we get killed. Let's go home now, Jeb."

He shook his head. "No. You go if you want. It's down

the mountain that way from here." He pointed behind him. "You'll get to the river."

They argued, but Jeb wouldn't give way. "All right then," she reasoned, "one of us can approach them. The other should wait to see what happens and go for help if it looks bad. And it better be you who goes for help because I'd never find my way back."

"No, you can't go to them," he said. "If anyone's going to be in trouble, it better be me. I'm used to it."

"Jeb, think about it—" she began, but he shouted her down.

"*No!* We'll both watch them. We won't just barge in. We'll watch and see if they look peaceful."

She raised her eyebrow.

"What's wrong?"

"If your Indians are so good at surviving in the woods without anyone knowing about them, they must know we're here with all the noise we've been making."

He frowned, thinking about it. "Yeah. So there's no point us trying to hide. I'll start climbing."

They started off again. She was tired, but she wasn't going to let him out of her sight. They climbed. At first it was easy to scrabble over the boulders that had fallen off the cliff, and crawl up the slabs of rock where moss and grasses and wiry little bushes grew in the cracks. Toeholds and fingerholds came often, and the incline wasn't that steep. But then the rock veered abruptly outward and only a spider could have clung to it—upside down.

"Here's where we're going to circle around back," Jeb said. "This is the head of the bird." He scuttled sideways, crab-like, and she followed cautiously. Once she looked down and realized that falling could scrape her skin off before she ever landed in a treetop way, way down below.

"About here's the back," Jeb said finally. He was poised against the rock with a sky full of fleecy clouds behind him. Below them was a rug of knobby green that undulated on and on as far as the eye followed it.

"I don't see any cornfields," she said.

"I better go up some more to get a better view," he said. "See that ledge? I'm going there."

"Jeb, it's too steep. Don't."

He was moving along the rock face, ignoring her. She held her breath in fear. Her feet were wedged into a wide crack, her arms splayed out for balance as she rested her cheek on the smooth rock hide. Her heart beat erratically as she watched Jeb getting higher in his vertical climb. His skinny butt hung out over empty space, and—where was he going? She bit her lip to hold back a scream as he scraped himself along, one foot in a crack, the rest of him on sheer rock, reaching, reaching.

Now he had a choice, around a corner and up onto the ledge or straight up along the line he'd been traveling. A shadow of a cloud covered him and she gasped. He'd chosen the corner. He seemed to her to be grasping it with his knees as he eased himself around it. If he fell, he wouldn't need any Indians to kill him—the rocks would do it.

"Jeb," she whispered. "Oh, Jeb." He was pulling himself onto the ledge, elbows out and legs dangling over the abyss. Then he was lying on the ledge, which seemed barely wide enough for his body. For a long time he rested. Finally, when she had grown impatient, he eased himself to his feet and stood with his back against the rock and his hands out for balance, looking down at the valley. From where he was standing, he could see half of New York State, she thought, but she didn't dare call to him. One startled movement and he'd fall.

"I don't see anything, Lexi," he said finally.

"Nothing?"

"Just trees."

"Well, then come down."

"I can't."

"Why?"

"I don't know how."

"Oh, God," she whispered to herself. "Then stay there," she yelled. "I'll go back and get help."

"You don't know the way."

"I'll find it." She'd go. Maybe she'd be lucky and stumble onto the river somehow. If she just headed down, found a stream, something. . . .

"I got up here. I guess I can get down." He sounded shaky. She saw him squat and begin easing himself back around the corner the way he had come, slowly, painfully slowly. Her own muscles trembled as she imagined how his must feel. Quietly she whimpered to herself. His leg extended out to one side, feeling for a toehold, reaching. She bit her lip. He drew back and tried again. He had it. The other leg. And then he slipped.

She screamed as he slid on his belly down the rock face. Her scream echoed over the valley, the empty valley. Not a soul was there to care about what happened to them. It was just Jeb and her and now he was hurt, caught on a bush that grew in one of the cracks. He lay very still.

She began easing herself along the rock face closer to him, at an angle, the way the crack went. It took her a long while and still he hadn't moved. But when she reached him he spoke to her.

"There's no Indians. I took you up here for nothing. There's no Indians, Lexi."

"Are you okay?" She could only see the side of him away from the rock and that looked normal, but when he turned, she saw the blood. His whole left side—face, arms, and probably his body under his jeans and T-shirt—was scraped. "Did you break any bones?"

"I don't know. It hurts all over. We got to get down somehow." He sounded desperate, but he began to move toward her. She backed down until she could let go of the crack she'd been clinging to like a lifeline and stand. They were close to the treetops now, and the rocks were sloped and walkable. He stood up gingerly.

"Okay?" she asked.

"Yeah, except my arm. I think I did something to it."

He looked awful, bloody and gray and brown with exhaustion and mud. "We'll get you home and to a doctor," she said. The Band-Aids were useless, but when they got to where they'd left the plastic bags, she spread the antiseptic cream as far as it would go over his visible wounds. He submitted in silence.

Without discussing it they began to make their way in the direction he had pointed toward, where he said the river was to be found. After a while it worried her that he wasn't talking. "Maybe we should rest for a while," she said, and added quickly, in case the idea offended his Indian courage, "because I'm tired."

He shook his head and kept going. She followed. "Jeb, say something," she said.

"I don't see why he lied to me," Jeb said.

She sighed and kept walking.

It seemed like a miracle when they emerged from the woods on the riverbank. They could hear the rapids, and she recognized the pool where they'd caught the fish. "I'm going to swim you across," she said. He didn't object. He let her lead him into the water. She told him how to lie and not to struggle and showed him in shallow water that she could grasp him under the chin and pull him along while she sidestroked with the other arm. The water only became too deep to wade across for a few feet in the middle. It was an easy crossing for her. They could have done this yesterday and been home, she thought, but she didn't say that to him. He got to his knees on the far bank and then to his feet.

"I'm sorry, Lexi. I'm really sorry," he said.

"About what?" she said. "So what if we didn't find any Indians. It was interesting and we survived, and that's what matters."

"But he lied."

"Trueblood?"

"That's why he didn't wake us up and take us home when you saw him last night. He didn't want to own up that he was a liar. He never saw any signs out there."

He sounded so bitter. She told him, "Jeb, you'll feel better tomorrow when you're not so tired," but he didn't seem to hear her. She felt helpless, because nothing she could say would pry him loose from his disappointment now, when he wasn't willing to be comforted.

11

They were silent crossing the railroad bridge. Above them, the clouds had piled up in ominous white and gray boulders, and in the distance thunder rumbled. They were trudging down the road toward home when a pick-up truck came racing toward them trailing a caterpillar of dust. The truck, driven by Uncle Jake, jerked to a stop. Jim and Joe leaped out of the back where they'd been holding a canoe in place.

"Where were you guys? We been looking all over for you. We figured you got drowned," Jim said.

"We didn't drown," Jeb said unnecessarily. "But we lost our food when the raft broke up down by the rapids."

140

"Your raft broke up? When?" Jim asked. "We just now borrowed this canoe to start looking for you."

"We were going to canoe upstream by the rapids," Joe said. By the downbeat in his and Jim's tone of voice, Lexi figured they were disappointed that their rescue mission was aborted.

She said, "Jeb and I camped out in the woods last night."

"I bet you were scared," Jim said, grinning at her.

"Lexi's not scared of anything," Jeb said loyally. "And she's great in the woods. She was the one caught the fish, and she made us blankets. . . . Oh, and she saved my life."

"Nice little detail you almost forgot there," Jim said. "So how did you save Jeb's life, Cousin?"

"It was nothing really."

"I bet," Jim said, but his grin wasn't mocking anymore.

"You don't look too good, Jeb," Uncle Jake said.

"I got scraped up climbing Bird Cliff. I think I did something to my arm."

"What were you climbing Bird Cliff for?" Now Jim sounded really impressed.

"Good thing we found you," Uncle Jake muttered before Jeb could answer. "The women been worried. You kids getting in the truck now?"

While Jeb eased himself into the cab, Jim asked Lexi again, "How'd you save his life?"

141

"I can swim and he can't. It was no big deal," Lexi said.

"You don't look like you been swimming much," Jim laughed.

Lexi touched her face which she'd only partially washed. "Anyway, the mud kept the mosquitoes from eating us alive," she said.

"You made blankets?" Joe sounded curious.

"We'll tell you all about it at home," Lexi said. She was impatient with them, standing there in the road asking questions when Jeb needed medical attention and both of them were hungry and exhausted.

The smell of home-baked bread made Lexi salivate as she entered the kitchen. To her amazement, she was grabbed and hugged, first by Janet, and then, not to be outdone, by Jesse.

"Thank God you're alive," Janet said. "We didn't want to have to tell your parents you were dead when you only just got here."

Aunt Jane came in. "I've been trying to reach your folks, Lexi, but I couldn't make the telephone operator understand me."

"Well, do they speak English in West Africa, Ma?" Jim asked.

"That telephone operator sure didn't. Not my kind of English anyway," Aunt Jane said. "You children must be starved. You didn't hurt yourselves? No broken bones or anything?" As she spoke, she finally focused on Jeb. "Jeb!" she cried. "What'd you do to yourself?"

"Fell," he said.

"Well, I better get you to the doctor. You look a mess."

"Can I have something to eat first, please?" Jeb said.

Immediately the women began rushing around the kitchen. Lexi sank into a chair at the table and asked for a glass of water, which Janet brought her. In short order the table was covered with food—chicken and cheese and ham and cold baked beans and potato salad and the bread that smelled so good. "I am starved," Lexi said. "All we had to eat was one little fish and some berries."

"Lexi saved my life," Jeb said again. At length they let him tell the tale. Jeb was a good storyteller. Dreamily Lexi relived the crack-up of their raft as Jeb took them down the rapids.

"But the paddles are gone. One I lost in the river and one we didn't bother lugging with us. And I had True-blood's bow and arrows, but I didn't shoot anything, but Lexi caught us a fish."

Even the boys listened patiently to the details of how Lexi had caught the sucker, and they acknowledged her ingenuity in suggesting tissues and wood shavings to start the fire.

"Smart girl," Aunt Jane said. "Looks like you know how to make the most of what you got." Judging by the tone of her aunt's voice, that was high praise.

"How did you make the blankets?" Joe asked again.

Lexi explained about taking the plastic garbage bags along, "just in case." And how it turned out they came in handy. She described the way they'd filled the bags and used them to insulate themselves against the cold.

"Smart girl," Aunt Jane said again. "I'm not surprised. Your dad was a sharp one in school, too."

"And Lexi's brave," Jeb attested.

"Jeb's the one," Lexi said. "Most of the stuff that we needed, he thought of, and he got us out of those woods."

"Well," Aunt Jane said. "The main thing is you're home and that's a relief. We had enough excitement around here thinking something terrible had happened to you."

Later, when Jeb returned from the local doctor with his arm in a sling and his scrapes cleaned up, Lexi asked him, "Are you going to talk to Trueblood?"

"What about?"

"To give him a chance to explain."

"I don't want to talk to him. Jim's going to take the bow and arrows back for me."

"Maybe Trueblood'll have a good explanation," Lexi said.

"I don't want to hear it," Jeb said.

"Jeb," she pointed out. "You don't have that many friends."

"Just you, and you're leaving at the end of the summer. I know."

"So?"

"So, I don't care." He went up to his room then. She let him be. His disappointment needed time to heal.

The next morning Lexi got two unexpected invitations. Jim asked her if she wanted to go to the ball field with Joe and him. "Not today," she said. "I have something I've got to do today that may take awhile."

"Well, do you like baseball?"

"I like soccer," she said.

"Maybe you'd be good," Jim said doubtfully. "We had a girl on our team last year."

She smiled. Sometime it might be fun to show him what she could do with a ball, but not today. She had made up her mind to get Jeb to give Trueblood a chance to explain.

The second invitation was from Janet, who was wrapping up some freshly baked bran muffins to take to their mother's friend.

"Jesse and me are going to go keep Ethel company. She's home from the hospital and she's lonesome. Want to come with us?"

"Ethel's a sketch," Jesse said. "She knows the plot of every soap by heart."

"Thanks," Lexi said. "But I have something to take care of that may take awhile."

"You're not going off on another camp-out, are you?" Janet asked Lexi.

Lexi laughed. "No. Not for a while, anyway."

"So what is it you've got to do?" Jesse asked.

"It's for Jeb."

"You already saved his life," Janet said.

"Did he come down for breakfast?" Lexi asked.

"No. Ma sent the boys up to find out if his arm was hurting him. He said he was fine, but he's still up in bed."

"That's weird," Jesse said. "Jeb's always out of the house as fast as he can get. And he *never* misses breakfast."

"I'll go see if I can find out what's wrong," Lexi said. She was pretty sure she knew already, but she put a glass of milk and two of the freshly baked muffins on a plate for him and went upstairs.

Jeb didn't answer her knock. "I'm bringing you breakfast in bed," she said through the closed door.

"Not hungry."

"Yes, you are. I hope you're decent because I'm coming in." She waited a minute. "Jeb?" No answer. She opened the door. He was lying face down under the covers with the pillow over his head, even though it was a warm, humid morning.

"Arm hurt?" she asked.

"No."

"Then what's wrong with you?"

"Nothing."

She put the plate down on the floor beside his bed. "Your sisters baked these. They're delicious."

No answer.

"I was hoping you'd go fishing with me."

"Not today."

"You mad at me about something?" she asked, knowing he wasn't, but hoping to rouse him.

He pulled the pillow off his head and, with some effort, rolled over so that he could look at her. His hair stuck out in all directions, and with his eyes going in separate directions as well, he looked funny. She grinned at him fondly.

"You know I'm not mad at you," he said.

"Then tell me what's wrong."

"Nothing."

"You're upset because Trueblood didn't let us know he came to our campsite?"

Jeb considered. "I'm mad about that, too, but what I can't swallow is he lied. There wasn't any Indians. He shouldn't of made me think there was."

"But he didn't do it to be mean, Jeb. He was just telling you a story. Maybe he half believed it himself. It was kind of exciting to think there might be Indians around still living in their old way."

"You don't lie to a friend."

"You took his bow and arrow," Lexi pointed out.

"That was different."

"I don't know," she said. "If you're not perfect, why do you expect him to be?"

He looked at the muffins and milk without interest and lay back down, turning away from her so that she couldn't see his face. "Aren't you going to get up?" she asked. No answer. "I need you to show me a good fishing spot," she said.

The stubborn line of his back remained unchanged. "Jeb? Won't you help me. *I'm* your friend."

"Please, leave me alone, Lexi."

She gave up temporarily and went downstairs to read and think. The big living room echoed with the family even as she sat alone in it. There were lint balls under the couch that Aunt Jane had overlooked and snips of thread Janet and Jesse had left. Just the way the chairs were positioned around the TV and the way the upholstery was dented from the shapes of their bodies echoed the family's presence.

Lexi was glad that her cousins seemed to like and respect her now, but that didn't make her one of them.

She was too different from them to belong to their tribe. She would never quite belong in this room. She would never quite fit in here. She understood now. No matter how fond they became of her and she of them, she would always stand a little apart—from all of them except Jeb.

She had been reading for over an hour when it occurred to her that if she couldn't budge Jeb, she might try moving Trueblood. She left a note, out of habit, to say where she was going and set off for the store.

The big man sat with his chair tilted on its back legs. He was whittling another turtle, she saw, when she said hello to him. It looked just like the one on the wall of his store.

"Where's Jeb?" Trueblood asked.

"He's upset."

"What about?"

"You. He says you lied to him."

"I never lied. I didn't say the Indians was there, just that they might be."

"You said you saw them."

"Signs. I never said I saw more than signs."

"Was there really a cornfield? Did you climb Bird Cliff and see one?"

"You a detective? Where's your warrant?"

"Well, you sent him on a wild goose chase, and he doesn't think you'd do that if you really liked him. He won't get out of bed. He's not eating."

"I should've known better than to let that kid hang around."

"But you encouraged him to. You must like him, True-blood."

"Sure I like him. Why not? . . . Customer told me he saw you go by on a raft, and when I found the paddle, I tracked you to your campfire. Don't that sound like I like the kid?"

"But why did you just go away after you found us?"

"You saw me?" He looked at her hard. "I thought you was asleep."

"You scared me," she said.

His shrug reminded her of Jeb. She wondered if Jeb had copied it. "Looked as if you were doing fine, and the river was only a quarter of a mile downhill. I figured you'd rather make it there on your own."

"Well, if you'd led us home, Jeb wouldn't have tried to climb that cliff."

"Yeah, Jim told me Jeb climbed Bird Cliff. I never thought he'd do that."

"Well, he did, and he fell. He could have been killed. As it is he's all scraped up and he's cracked a bone in his arm."

"Fool kid. I never thought he'd try. It scared *me* when I climbed it."

So he had done that much. "And what did you see from the top?"

"Nothing," Trueblood said. "I never got to the top."

"Then it was a lie about the cornfield?"

Trueblood squirmed. "You kept badgering me about how to find them Indians. I don't know what made me think of a cornfield. I got carried away."

"Please," she said. "Come to the house and tell him you weren't trying to make a fool of him. Please!"

"I can't leave the store. You bring him here. Tell him I got something for him."

"What?" she asked.

"You'll see if you bring him."

"*Are* you his friend?" she asked.

"I got no friends," Trueblood said grimly. "Never had." Grudgingly he added, "But Jeb's okay. Bring him here. You'll see."

12

Persuading Jeb that he had to get out of bed and go see Trueblood was not easy. At first, he didn't even seem to be listening. Lexi finally got angry and shook his shoulder. "Jeb, what's the matter with you? I thought you were a fair person. It's only fair to give Trueblood a chance to explain."

"There weren't any Indians, Lexi. How's he going to explain that?"

"Listen, suppose they had been there, and suppose they wanted to adopt you like you said. How long would you have stayed with them?"

"I don't know. Till I grew up."

"You'd live in the woods and be cold and hungry and not have anything to read and not see your family for years and years?"

"You said you were willing."

"But I wasn't thinking for years. I thought maybe just to see what it was like, and then I'd leave. I love my parents. And even if I didn't, I'd want to go to school and learn and check books out of a library and read. I'd want to see what happens in this world."

He took a deep breath and thought for a while, staring at his knees. Then he said, "I guess for me the stars would be enough."

"The stars?"

"You know, at night, sleeping out in the woods. I wouldn't mind so much being cold and hungry. . . . I really wanted to be an Indian."

She squeezed his hand in sympathy, but she couldn't think of what to say until she remembered what Trueblood had said. "He wants to give you something. Don't you want to find out what it is?"

"No," Jeb said. "I'm finished being his friend."

She was tired of trying to persuade him and ready to give up, but Trueblood had said he had no friends. The Indian was as lonely as Jeb. They needed each other. She sighed and made one last effort. "Jeb, I want to see what he's going to give you. Come for my sake, please."

It was her weakest argument, but somehow, it was the winning one.

Jeb would have stayed silent all the way to the store, but she chatted to cheer him up. "As soon as your arm heals, you ought to let me teach you to swim, Jeb. Everybody should know how, and you live by a river. Besides, we don't have anything more important to do now except go fishing. Oh, and I still want to explore the woods around here. Would you go with me?"

"What about Janet and Jesse?" he asked.

"What about them?"

"I thought you wanted to hang out with them."

"Well, I changed my mind. You're the only one here I really fit with."

"I don't fit with anyone."

"Yes, you do. With me."

"But you'll leave at the end of the summer," he said mournfully.

"That won't change how we feel about each other," she said.

"How can you be friends with somebody far away?"

"It'll be hard," she said, "the way everything is for us

because we're different, but that's okay. I'd rather be the way I am than like everybody else."

"You would? But I thought—"

"I changed my mind," she said. "That night in the woods, I started thinking. I like myself fine the way I am. Why should I change to make people accept me?"

"So that you won't be lonely."

"Being lonely's not so bad. We can deal with it."

"I don't know," he said.

"We *have* to deal with it, Jeb. It's part of how we are." She wished she could convince him, but the store was in sight. Trueblood was sitting in his chair watching them come. Jeb's eyes met Trueblood's and locked.

"Why did you lie to me?" Jeb asked straight out.

"I didn't lie."

"I nearly got killed on Bird Cliff."

"How was I to know you'd be fool enough to try and climb it?" Trueblood sounded indignant. "I knew you had guts, but I didn't think you was crazy."

"It's like people making little kids believe in Santa Claus. You fooled me like I was a little kid," Jeb said.

Trueblood groaned. "Listen, I didn't mean to fool you. I liked teaching you that Indian stuff. I thought I was the only one cared until. . . . Hey, if I knew you'd get so mad, I wouldn't of told you nothing. . . . Hey, don't *I* got a right to make mistakes?"

155

Jeb considered his sneakers. Then he looked over one shoulder at the tree. Finally he looked back at Trueblood and shrugged. Trueblood smiled his lopsided smile. He put his hand on Jeb's shoulder and said, "Got something for you." Up came Trueblood's other hand with a crudely carved turtle in it.

Jeb's eyes went to the turtle affixed to the siding next to the door. "The one you're giving me's not a real clan sign, is it?" Jeb asked.

"Why not?" Trueblood asked slyly. "An Indian made it."

"You're just half Indian," Jeb said.

"That's the most you're going to find in these parts. You want it or not?"

"It doesn't mean anything," Jeb muttered, looking at the ground.

"It means you and me are the same clan now," Trueblood said. He squeezed Jeb's shoulder, but Jeb shook Trueblood's hand off and muttered something. "What?" Trueblood asked.

"I said, a liar's clan," Jeb said.

Lexi had been listening in silence. Now she put in, "Jeb, he didn't lie exactly, no more than you stole when you took the bow and arrows without asking. He wants to be your friend. He's different, too, Jeb."

"It don't matter," Trueblood said. "If he wants to stay mad at me, let him stay mad."

They were both so touchy, Lexi thought. Under the wicked scars, Trueblood was as much a boy as Jeb was. "Jeb," she said sharply and pushed him.

"Okay. Okay," Jeb said. He looked up at the big Indian and asked, "So where should I hang it? Over my bed or something?"

"That'd be good," Trueblood said. Their smiles latched and held.

On the way home Jeb said, "You don't even like him much. Why'd you want us to make up?"

"Well. . ." She thought about it. "Because when people like us *do* find a friend, we have to hang on to him. We don't need to be lonely all the time, Jeb."

He smiled at her and sniffed. "You got an answer for everything, Lexi."

A bird flashed dark across the road and gave a call like liquid music. "What's that?" she asked.

"Red-winged blackbird. Lots of them around here."

"You're lucky."

"Yeah," he said, and then he said. "I guess we could go fishing, but with my arm tied up, you'll have to bait the hooks."

"Fine with me. I'm a good hook baiter," she said.

The day was warm. The sky was blue. They were going

fishing. Lexi's spirit sang with the blackbird's liquid music. Ezekiel, can you hear me, she thought. I am walking with a friend toward a riverbank with a swift-flowing stream to go fishing, and I am happy, Ezekiel. I am happy to be part of this earth to which I belong.